MW01366667

# Julienna

Victor's Story

Written By: Betty Keller
Co-Written By: Sylvia Nichols

# Books

Julienna-( Book 1): Is about a young woman trapped in an arranged marriage. She falls in love with another man. Will she honor her parents wishes and marry Aiden Crawford or will she marry Victor Wolf the man with secrets.

Julienna- Victor's Story-( Book 2): is an engaging story of Victor Wolf's point of view and how his life changes dramatically from a young child to a teenager as he finds out that he is a werewolf. His love and loss for friends down to having to leave and go into hiding to protect the people he cares for. His point of view takes on a new life as it describes how he feels when he first sees Julienna and where it goes from there.

# Introduction

“I’m a werewolf...” Victor leaned into Julienna’s ear and whispered as tears filled his eyes.
“You're the beast!? A werewolf?” Julienna exclaimed as she covered her mouth with her hands.
“As are you now... my love.” Victor said knowingly as a tear fell from his eye onto his cheek.
“But how? I mean when did you know?” Asked Julienna.
“It's a long story that begins many years ago.” Said Victor as he wiped away his tears.

Two boys were playing in the snow. Chasing each other and throwing snowballs. Both laughing the more they ran. Victor was almost five years old. He had light brown hair and chocolate brown eyes with a red tint to them. The boy he played with was almost four. He had dirty blond hair and green eyes that shined like emeralds. As both laughed and played Victor jumped upon the boy by accident.
“You need to be more careful before you hurt someone, child.” The woman pulled him off and scolded him.
“I am sorry Ma’am. I tripped in the snow.” Victor explained as he pointed at a large pile of snow. Another woman came out and lifted Victor off the ground. His mother Lenore Wolf.

“Mama I wanna play with my friend.” Victor said as he struggled in his mother’s arms. The other little boy ran up to the other woman.

“Mommy I am not hurt. Why must they leave?” Aiden asked his mother Alice Crawford.

“My darling son they are different. There is no place for their kind among ours.” Aiden’s mother knelt to the ground and explained. She then took his hand and took the boy inside the house. Each of the boys looked for the other amongst the snow. Then it began to snow heavily and the wind began to gust. They never saw each other again.

# Chapter 1

Lenore was in a cottage within the woods that her former lover gave her for her son Victor. It was a quaint cottage. Just big enough for the two of them.

"I am sorry I can't take the boy Lenore. My wife has forbidden it." Aaron Crawford explained.

"Alice is incompinet. The boys got along wonderfully and if our plan had worked they would have grown up together, loved." Lenore said exasperated.

"You have this cottage for now for the boy. I will have another in a few weeks out of town for you both since you must leave." Aaron took her by the hand. He then handed her a large purse with coin within it.

"I don't want your money Aaron. I want our son to be raised with his brother!" Lenore exclaimed, now becoming desperate.

"You know I can not allow it. Alice…" Aaron tried to argue his point but was interrupted.

"I care not for Alice. She has taken everything. Rip out my heart so that you know how I feel!" Lenore yelled at him as she began to cry.

"Mama?? Are you okay?" A sleepy Victor walked out from the bedroom rubbing his eyes.

“Mama’s fine my darling boy. The nice man was just leaving.” Lenore explained softly to her son as she picked him up and showed Aaron to the door.
“Thank you for what you HAVE done for us Sir.” Lenore said sternly as she held the door open.
“Write to me if you need anything else Madam.” Aaron tipped his hat to them and left in the cold night snow. Lenore took Victor back to the bedroom and laid him in his bed. Victor yawned and fell back to sleep. Lenore walked to the window and looked to the night sky. She grabbed her shawl and ran outside. Aaron hadn’t gotten very far.
“I am sorry I was cross.Please come back until the storm passes.” Lenore invited him back. Aaron followed and sat at the table.
“Why invite me back Lenore? You made your point quite plain.” Aaron boomed.
“Because you kept a roof over our heads. I want our son to come to you if he needs to some day.” Lenore explained. Aaron sat there for a moment still trying to get warm.
“And what else do you want? You’re up to something.” Aaron said as he gave her a cautious look.
“I need a nanny. One that will not talk about us. They must keep us a secret at all times.” Lenore demanded.
“Ah Yes, the full moon.” Aaron gasped.
“It is becoming harder to hide it from Victor.” Lenore explained.
“Yes, I would assume. I will figure out something within the next few days.” Aaron said as he yawned.
“Thank you Aaron.” Lenore said as tears streamed from her eyes again.
“Of course but I am becoming tired. I will be stealing the sofa until the storm passes. Goodnight.” Aaron boomed again with a loud yawn and a thud upon the sofa. Within moments he was asleep.

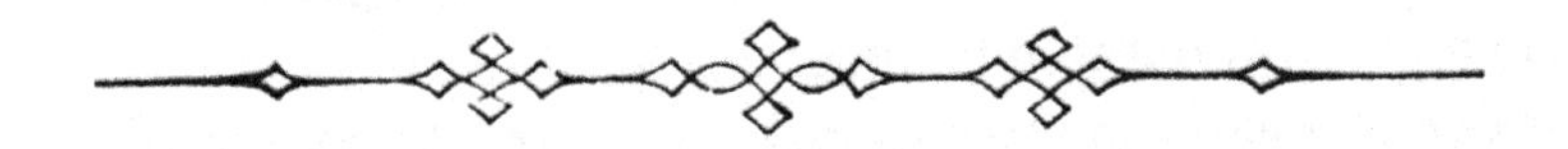

# Chapter 2

Victor had been outside playing with some branches. Building a miniature cabin it seemed. The nanny looked over at him and smiled while she was staying in the open doorway. As the Nanny changed direction she saw a beast run towards them.

"Victor! Run into the house! Now!" The nanny yelled. Victor hurried and ran into the house and hid in his bedroom. The Nanny frantically shut the door. But it was too late. The beast had made it inside. Victor saw the open window and jumped out of it. He ran as far as his legs would carry him. He heard the nanny screaming. He refused to look back. When he could hear no more screaming he stopped. He hunched over to catch his breath. He looked away and saw a woman.

"Miss! Miss! Please Help me!" He shouted. The lady walked up to him.

"Then who will help me?!" The woman exclaimed. She fell over covered in her own blood. He panicked and ran. He ran straight into his mother.
"Victor. There you are darling. Come now we must go." Lenore picked up the boy. She was very calm all though covered in blood. Victor's breathing returned to almost normal as he fell asleep in his mother's arms. Lenore had a carriage waiting. As she approached the carriage holding Victor in her arms the driver noticed she was covered in blood.
"Do ya need help Madam? The child?" The driver spoke panaked.
"The beast did not get him. We just need to leave." Lenore spoke softly as she climbed upon the carriage still grasping Victor.
"Where to Madam?" Asked the driver.
"Hecla." Lenore simply answered as she laid Victor down on her lap.
"Hecla it is then Madam." The driver answered, then yelled to the horse. It was a long ride. Several days journey from White River South Dakota. They had an occasional stop here and there so that they could eat or take care of business. Victor did school work while riding with his mother.
"Ms. Wolf, we need to stop here so that I may get some rest." The driver explained as he yawned wide and pulled into an inn.
"You will pay for your own room. At this rate we will never get there." Stated Lenore as she rolled her eyes. The driver said nothing as he walked his horses to the post and tied them up. He then walked into the inn to pay for his room. Lenore and Victor followed. Victor held his mother's hand. The inn was quite large. It was a log cabin, as they first walked in there was a huge white stone fireplace. To the left

was a dining room and kitchen. On the right there were three bedrooms for rent. In front of the fireplace there was a wingback chair and a sofa. Victor sat in the chair and played with toys there in the room while Lenore checked in. After being given a skeleton key for the room Lenore took Victor by the hand and led him to the room.

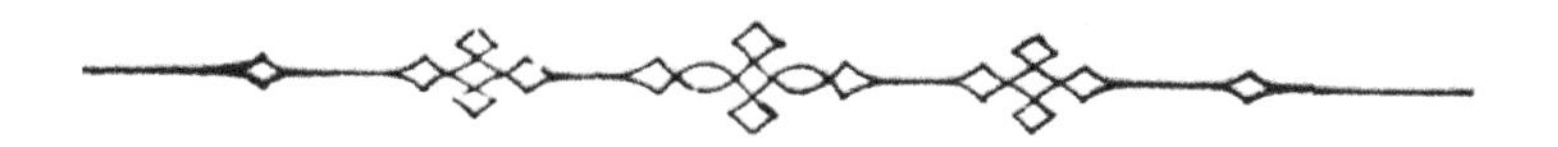

# Chapter 3

A few days later they arrived at the house in Hecla Nebraska. The leaves were just budding on the giant maple tree in front of the house.
"Mama, where are we?" Victor asked.
"This is our new home son." Lenore explained as they walked in the house. The driver brought the luggage inside the doorway.
"Nice place here Madam. Did your husband hit the gold mines?" The driver asked curiously as he held out his hand for payment.
"Unfortunately he didn't." Lenore said as she handed the man a handful of gold coins. The driver closed his hand around the coins. Tipped his hat and left. The house was very nice. It was a whitewashed brick Victorian with a wrap-around patio.
"A red door. That will have to go." Exclaimed Lenore to herself. She showed Victor his room with all sorts of toys and then proceeded to unpack things. It wasn't long before a knock came to the door. Lenore ignored it. Then the knock came again.

“Can I help you?!” Lenore flew the door open and asked, agitated.
“Good day Ma’am. I noticed you are in the Crawford home. If there's anything I can do for you please let me know.” Said the excited short man. Lenore thought for a moment.
“I was going to put an advertisement in the paper but I am in need of a servant and a nanny.” Lenore explained.
“I will get the message out promptly Ma’am.” The short man said.
“I am Ms. Wolf, Lenore What may I call you?” Lenore stated.
“The name’s Kelsey Ma’am. Jonathan Kelsey.” Said Jonathan.
“Mama I’m hungry.” Victor walked up to his mother.
“Hello little one.” Jonathan said as he pulled a piece of silver from his pocket and handed it to the child. Victor instantly dropped it. Lenore pulled him back and shut the door. Her eyes are fierce red. She looked at his hand. It was burnt.
“Go into the kitchen. I will be right there.” Lenore said sternly to Victor. As she composed herself she opened the door.
“I am sorry. My son is allergic to that metal.” Lenore explained as she handed the piece of silver back.
“But thank you again for your attention, If you’ll excuse me.” Lenore stated.
“Yes Ma’am, Ms. Lenore. I am sorry about the silver…” Jonathan said as Lenore shut the door on him and proceeded to the kitchen to fix Victor some food.

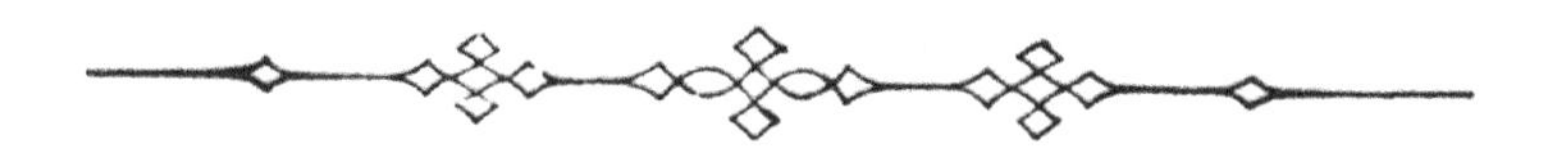

## A few years later...

Aaron,

I worry about Victor. His temper has the best of him. I am worried it will awaken the beast within him and the worse part is that he will not be able to control it. I feel as we will need to talk soon about his social standing. I fear it will affect his ability to prepare for high society in the next couple years. I am not sure what I can do, having been an outcast myself. Please return word so I may decide which way I shall turn!

# Chapter 4

"Aaron there was no reason to come all the way out here." Lenore exclaimed.

"He is changing according to your letter is he not?" Aaron argued.

"He has my dysfunction, it is true but if we want him in society he needs proper tutors if we wish for him to be any kind of civilized." Lenore argued back. Aaron reached into his pocket and pulled out a handkerchief and wiped his brow.

"How much are we talking about Lenore? I have minors in the gold mine working day and night." Aaron started to get frustrated.

"Aaron this isn't about money. It's about his social standing. If we are to find the boy a good..." Lenore tried to mislead him.

"What of MY NAME! You refused to give MY SON MY NAME!" Aaron exclaimed as he stood and knocked the table over.

Lenore was speechless as she looked past Aaron in rage. You could see what appeared to be her blood boiling. Her eyes begin to glow red.
"You were with your wife. And you made it quite clear that YOUR name was not going to be put on MY SON."
"Your right my wife was the reason I could not claim him being born a bastard." Aaron backed down.
"*He will be sixteen next week. He needs the high class society so he may be ready by seventeen*!" Lenore asked again.
" You have given him one year to prepare to meet a potential bride in what takes a lifetime ." Aaron placed another large purse in front of Lenore filled with five times the normal amount of coin. Lenore snatched the bag and placed it upon her chest.
"Be careful who you trust around here. Every rose has it's thorn . A suggestion for you is to use Marie Kelsey, she is the best although expensive." Aaron shuddered thinking about the cost as he got up to leave. Lenore followed him out onto the patio. A boy ran past him. He stopped when he saw Aaron.
"Sir." Victor tilted his head then kissed his mother on her check as he ran into the house.
"Make sure he shaves and gets a haircut. He's awful...rugged." Exclaimed, Aaron as he handed Lenore another small handful of coins. Lenore nodded her head and watched him leave. She walked back into the house and took the money into her room.
"Mama, I'm going to go out to the old mines." Victor yelled as he ran out of the house and slammed the door.
"Victor…" Lenore yelled but realized he was already gone. Lenore decided a few hours later that she was going to go to the market and talk to Jonathan Kelsey. Perhaps he could point her in the correct direction.

“Victor go get the water pitcher and basin and wash up well. We are going into town.” Lenore said to her son when he came waltzing back in the door covered from head to toe in dirt.
“Mama really? I do not want to go anywhere!” Victor whined as he stomped his feet.
“NOW!!” Lenore growled. Victor knew how serious she was and went to wash and change his clothes. Lenore also went and changed and washed up. When she was done she grabbed a small change purse.
“Mama I’m ready.” Victor said as he rolled his eyes.
“Out the door then. It’ll be a nice walk.” Lenore exclaimed.
“WALK, what's wrong with the horses.” Victor whined again.
“There is nothing wrong with the horses. You just cleaned up. NOW WALK!” Lenore was now growing frustrated. Victor hestintly obeyed his mother. Following behind her kicking at stones all the way.
“Victor! Really?!” His mother exclaimed agitated.
“What?! I don’t want to do this!” Victor yelled back. Lenore grew more and more angry but kept it under control. As they approached the market they discovered it was very busy. Lenore approached the barber Guessepi.
“Afternoon Sir.” Lenore greeted Guessepi. He glanced at Lenore and grinned.
“Afternoon Madam. What can I do for you?” He looked up and released his client. Lenore pulled Victor in front of them. The barber looked as he was in shock.
“How much to make him look like a gentleman?” Lenore asked briskly. The barber thought for a moment before he answered.
“Five pieces of silver or two gold pieces for a haircut only.” The barber came back.
“Three pieces of gold for a nice gentleman's haircut and a shave with sideburns short and neat.” Lenore bartered.

"You know how to make a deal. All right. Done." Smiled the barber as Lenore gave him the three pieces of gold. Victor sat down and was slightly nervous. As the barber worked on Victor, Lenore walked around the market looking for Jonathan Kelsey. She knew he had a shop around where he sold vegetables and such. She ended up finding him more to the edge of the market.

"Good Afternoon." Lenore greeted him as she purchased tomatoes and lettuce from him.

"Afternoon. Will there be anything else today? Are y'all in the market for some meat? We just butchered a cow this mornin'." Jonathan exclaimed loudly.

"No, no meat today but I am looking for someone and thought that you may know her." Lenore said as she paid for the vegetables.

"Who ya lookin fer?" Jonathan asked as he closed one eye and put his hand to his chin. Lenore told him who she was in search of.

"Marie? Yes I believe it was Marie Kelsey. It is said she does social grooming." Lenore asked.

"OH yeah I reckon I know her. Tough old bird she is." Jonathan boisterd loudley.

"You do?" exclaimed Lenore happily.

"Well I dang well better. She be me wife." Jonathan smiled wide as he was still very loud. He pointed over to a tall woman with long blond hair hiding behind a white brimmed hat. Lenore placed her hand upon her heart. She did not see that one coming. Jonathan was a rather short man approximately five feet four inches tall and he was stout.. While his wife was six feet tall and was rather skinny. You would never pair these two in a crowd.

"Thank you Jonathan." Lenore said as she walked over to Marie. She stopped just short of her glancing over to see if her son was done looking like an animal. She signaled him

to come over as she saw he looked very much like a gentleman.
"Hello. May I help you." Marie asked Lenore.
"Yes. I was told that you could help me to groom my son into a gentleman." Lenore looked for the proper word as Victor walked over and stopped at the tall woman.
"Is this the boy we are speaking of?" asked Marie as she circled him like a vulture and looked back to Lenore.
"This is my son Victor Wolf. What will need to be done?" Lenore asked as she introduced him.
"My dear he is older and will have to learn fast. He should have been enrolled at least ten years ago." Marie said matter of factly.
"How much Marie? Money is no object." Lenore exclaimed as she urged her to write down the price. Marie took the paper and scribbled a number on it and folded it in half. She then handed it back to Lenore. Lenore took the paper and excused herself. Victor followed behind her looking over her shoulder as she opened the paper and read it.
"Mama there is NO WAY you can afford this." Victor exclaimed much louder than Lenore would have preferred. She turned and glared at her son.
"Is there a problem with the price? After all you said money is no object." Marie chorted.
"My finances are not my son's concern. This price is high but does it cover one year?" Lenore asked as she held the paper in her hand.
"That price is for one month." Marie smiled.
"That is outrageous. Just because we have the funds doesn't mean that we are going to pay that much!" Lenore exclaimed angrily.
"What's all the fussin' going on here." Came Jonathan's loud boisterous voice. Then Jonathan took the paper from Lenore's hand and looked at it.

"Marie, these people pay for a lot of beef from us. This price will be knocked in half!" Jonathan shouted.

"Jonathan that's not necessary." Lenore explained.

"Your price is half this number. When do you need it done?" Jonathan asked Lenore while glaring at his wife.

"One year." Lenore said.

"Done. Boy stop calling your mother Mama. It's disrespectful due to your age." Jonathan said first to Lenore then turned to Victor.

"Yes Sir." Stated Victor.

"Victor be to my house tomorrow morning promptly at eight am; you must be bathed and shaved. Your mother will bring you." Marie explained

# Chapter 5

The next morning Victor was up on his own. He had taken a bath and shaved his face. Everything except his sideburns. While his hair was still damp he had combed it back into a low ponytail. He then dressed in his sunday best. A dark brown suit with a white button up top. By seven thirty his mother was ready to leave by carriage and go to Kelsey manor.

"You're wearing that?" Lenore asked Victor.

"Due to the hour this is what I must wear...correct Mother?" Victor said smugly.

"I suppose so. Had you only gotten ready earlier you...". Lenore trails

"Come now into the carriage." She says as she opens the door. Victor climbed into the carriage and slouched down in the seat, lifted his onto the other seat and crossed his legs. Lenore got into the carriage and sat down. She glared at her son with his feet up. Victor rolled his eyes and huffed at her.

"Are you going to put your feet down?" Lenore asked Victor as she swatted his feet.

"Must you behave as a dog?" Lenore now is annoyed at Victor's lack of respect.

“NO!”he snarled, half joking and half feeling as if he had growled under his breath like just that of a dog.
“It’s not hurting you.” His eyes started to streak red as he grew agitated. Lenore gasped as she held her head down. After a short while the carriage finally arrived at the Kelsey manor. A hand appeared within the open door. Lenore came out holding a young gentleman's hand. Victor stomped out from the carriage.
" Oh, NO Sir. Back in that carriage. Daniel will show you the proper way to exit a carriage until you have it right." Marie Kelsey exclaimed as she twirled her finger. Victor scuffed as he rolled his eyes and got back into the carriage.
"You may bring him back into the manor when he understands carriage manors." Explained Marie. Daniel had explained to Victor that this was a boarding school and that he would most likely be staying there, while Victor really didn’t mind he was kind of worried of what his mother would do. Marie and Lenore then walked into the manor together. As they walked into the foyer a man came up and took their cloaks. He then escorted them to the sitting room. Marie and Lenore sat on the sofa in the parlor. The fireplace was lit but not roaring.
“Lenore, this may not be easy to hear....” Marie started to say as she handed her a cup of tea. Lenore and Marie engaged in some small talk, the usual how do you do. Having a feeling like something was not being said and not being one to beat around the bush Lenore pressed.
“What is it?” Lenore asked, taking a sip. Marie took a sip as well as she took a long second to glance over her tea cup at Lenore then set it down.
“Victor will be staying at the manor for the next year and a half.” Marie explained as she set her cup down.
“NO. Absolutely not. He is all that I have.” Lenore yelled as she slammed her tea cup down upon the table.

"Lenore this is a boarding school for young socialites. That's why it is so expensive." Marie explained as she put her hand upon Lenore's shoulder.
"We live just down the road! Why can't the carriage pick him up?" Lenore asked as she moved Marie's hand.
"It just isn't done that way. I will show you his room and you may stay upon the grounds for the day." Marie exclaimed. Lenore was about to argue with her but decided against it because it was for his benefit. Lenore agreed and Marie took her on a tour of the grounds. They walked out to the court and Marie began to show her where Victor and the other young socialites would have carriage duty and tend to the horses. Making their rounds they walked to the gardens where they ran into a ravishing young lady.
"Aunt Marie I have something for you." Said the teenage girl with long blond hair and green eyes as she handed her a flower. Marie took it and turned the girl to face Lenore.
"Ms. Wolf, this is our niece Rebekah Kelsey." Marie introduced her.
"Pleased to meet you Ms. Wolf." Rebekah curtsied. Lenore curtsied back and smiled continuing on with the tour. When they began to come into the manor the boys caught up with them and joined them. Lenore and Victor stayed for dinner upon finishing Lenore was being pushed to leave her son and quickly say their goodbyes.
"We will send for some of his things." Said Marie
"Write to me my son." Lenore exclaimed as she raised her hand to her son's face with tears welling in his eyes.
"Yes Mama; Mother. I promise." Victor said as he moved her hand and hugged her. He then walked her out to the carriage and properly helped her board her carriage. Upon Lenore's departure Marie would show Victor to his room.

# Chapter 6

***About nine months later:***

Sitting at the desk listening to Mrs. Kelsey, Victor couldn't help his mind wandering. He kept thinking about his mother and missing his own room and hanging out with his friends.
"Victor, can you please demonstrate how to do a proper introduction to a lady." Victor was thrown off as Mrs. Kelsey called upon him.
"Ummm yes Ma'am." Victor exclaimed as he stood and walked to the front of the class. He introduced himself to Mrs. Kelsey as he took her hand and bowed.
“Very good. I'm glad you were paying attention.” She said as she pulled her hand away and motioned Victor back to his seat. He followed her outstretched hand and sat back down.

After the day had been dragged out Victor and Daniel decided to go out amongst the ranch. They were walking past the horses as one of the girls ran up to them.
“Hello Daniel.” The girl swung her dress as she giggled.

"Hello Rebekah. How was school today?" Daniel asked the fourteen year old.
"Today was good but I miss my sister Anna at home." Rebekah said sadly.
"I am sorry. When do you see her again?" Daniel asked her as Victor was looking around bored.
"I'm gonna go back to the room." Victor interrupted. Daniel nodded his head as he finished his conversation. Back in the room Victor was throwing clothes around.
"Come on where are you?!" Victor groaned as he threw a basin and pitcher. They smashed against the door as Dainel walked in. He ducked fast. Glass just missed hitting him.
"What in the world are you doing?" Daniel shouted as he dared not move.
"Looking for something!" Victor growled back to him.
"And that would be...what?!" Daniel asked again as the school books were now being thrown. One went whizzing by Daniel's head.
"My pocket watch." Victor huffed as he now tore apart the beds.
"Is this it?" Daniel asked as he pulled a pocket watch from the top shelf of Victor's dresser. Victor stopped what he was doing to look. He tore the gold watch from Daniel's hand.
"What are you doing with this?" Victor exclaimed as he put the watch in his pocket. Then grabbed Daniel and held him to the wall. A low growl formed in his throat as he glared at Daniel.
"What is wrong with you?" Daniel struggled to say as he fought against Victor's grip around his neck.
"I'm...ahhh I'm… so sorry?" Victor stuttered as he lost his grip on Daniel. Daniel fell to the ground and was gasping for his breath. Still pulling himself up right against the wall.

"Daniel, Daniel???" Victor was in front of him. When Daniel finally caught his breath he sat up against the wall and closed his eyes. He put his hand up to stop Victor calling his name.
"Victor I'm fine. Why is that watch so important?" Daniel pointed to Victor's pocket.
"It was my father's. It's the only thing I have from him." Victor explained as he pulled the solid gold pocket watch from his pocket. As he opened it the sun gleamed on the fine words within. *'Control the beast within'.*
"What does that mean?" Daniel asked puzzled.
"I have never figured it out. But the watch works as it should and it is solid gold." Victor explained as he turned the key and moved the watch from hand to hand. After he was done with it, he dropped it back within his pocket. He stood and reached his hand out to help Daniel up. Daniel took it and stood with him.
"No hard feelings my friend?" Victor said apologetically as he held out his hand.
"No. Just control your temper. Let's clean up this mess before Mrs. Kelsey comes around." Daniel said calmly.
Both boys went around the room cleaning up. Returning the clothes and organizing. About the time they quit it was dark out. Dark enough to see the full moon through the window.
Daniel never quite understood why Victor was always so angry around this time. It was only a pocket watch Daniel thought as he slowly fell asleep.

~Victor's Dream~

A wolf was running through the woods. Dodging trees and chasing something. Seeing the scenery whipping past him. Victor knew if he could only gain enough speed he could catch up to the wolf. Victor jumped in his sleep as the wolf

turned and looked at him and turned back. A carriage appeared in front of the wolf stopping it in its tracks just short of the carriage. Out of nowhere there was a man in the distance yelling for help waving a lantern back and forth trying to get Victor's attention. It was like Victor was watching from above.
"LOOK OUT! BEHIND YOU!" Screamed a woman's voice coming from the carriage. The man with the lantern turned quickly although he was not quick enough to evade being mauled by the beast. The female in the carriage and driver took off to avoid becoming the beast snack. They both ran in separate directions to confuse the beast and throw him off their trail. Running in the brush in a large circle trying to avoid leaving her, the female made her way back to the carriage hoping the driver was still alive. She started to hear scratching at the carriage door. She didn't know what to do. She felt like she was trapped. Hearing the wolf snarling and growling she tried to scream for help. Then it dawned on her that she was alone and no one could hear her screams. She could see the wolf in plain view. Staring into the red/amber glow of his eyes. Suddenly it lunged at the woman.

# Chapter 7

"VICTOR! DANIEL! GET UP! YOUR LATE!" Shouted an angry Jonathan Kelsey. Both boys shot straight out of bed, tripping over some of the clothes they left on the floor from last night. Victor in a cold sweat from the nightmare he just had.

"HAVE Y'ALL BEEN IN THE WINE AGAIN?! MOVE IT!" Jonathan shouted again this time stomping the floor. The boys stumble trying to put on their undergarments, tripping on the clothes still on the floor from the tussle the night before.Standing in their undergarments trying to wake from the shock they had.

"On our way Sir." Both said as they watched him leave. Victor was throwing clothes around again to find his uniforms as Daniel was rubbing his eyes.

"This one is yours." Daniel said as he tossed the trousers to Victor. Both were dressed and they ran down the stairs to their next class.

"At least this one is easy." Stated Victor vaguely thinking about the dream the night before.

"It's too easy. I hate this class. Any idiot can help a noble girl from a carriage." Exclaimed Daniel.
"But me…?" Victor questioned as he looked towards Daniel.
"That's not what I said." Daniel defended himself.
"It's fine, let's get this over with." Victor stated as they approached the awaiting carriages for the maiden ball. Victor held the door open as Daniel reached in to receive a hand. A lovely woman came out of the carriage to be followed by her suiter. Then Daniel held the door open of another carriage while Victor reached in to receive a hand. The hand Victor received was cold and clammy. He shuddered at the feel of it. Daniel stifled a laugh. Victor shot a look at him and cleared his throat. No one came out of the carriage.
"Driver, who is in this carriage?" Shouted a confused Daniel. Victor had already walked into the carriage to find the suitor dead and the woman dying.
"Fetch Mr. Kelsey! NOW!" Shouted Victor to Daniel. The driver came to the door and looked in to see Victor covered in their blood.
"Boy what did you do?" The driver accused Victor.
"I did nothing. WHO are these people?" Victor asked angry that the driver had the nerve to blame him.
"This is Lord Sussex and his Fiance." Explained the driver. He began to sweat and wiped his brow with a handkerchief.
"Did anyone stop you on the way here?" Asked Victor. Just then he heard a cough. The lady was gasping for air. As Victor tried to get her head up Daniel and Jonathan had arrived.
"Out of the way!" Jonathan pushed them aside. Jonathan not being a thin man bust through the two. He and Daniel had pulled the frail woman out and boarded her onto an open carriage that was used to take her to the sick bay for the school. The boys and driver watched as the carriage left

with her and as others pulled the body of Lord Sussex out of the carriage. A mortician was then called to take his body.
"Again..." Shouted Jonathan to the driver.
"The road was flooded and we were to go through the woods last night. No one stopped us but the beasts surrounded us. We hit a fallen tree and Lord Sussex decided to look for help." The driver said plainly.
"And the fiance? Francis? What of her?" Asked Marie Kelsey.
"I sat with her Ma'am. She worried the whole time. She kept complaining of the wolves." Exclaimed the driver.
"What did you do to her! Did you touch her!?" Jonathan shouted at him.
"NO. I DIDN'T DO ANYTHING TO THE POMPAS WOMAN!" Shouted the driver now clearly angry. Jonathan and Marie now walked over to the boys who had been watching from a distance.
"Did anything seem off?" He whispered to them.
"Only the initial situation." Stated Daniel.
"No one else mentioned the road being flooded. Perhaps he's lying about other things as well." Suggested Victor.
"Perhaps, but for now we will send for the constable to deal with him." Whispered Jonathan.
"And a doctor for Lady Francis since the school is not equipped to handle this." Added Marie. Jonathan nodded and sent Daniel to notify them.
"Victor I am going to send you home for a couple of days to relax after all of this has happened." Exclaimed Marie.
"Mrs. Kelsey I am fine." Victor insisted.
"You will take MY CARRIAGE HOME now." Explained Marie.
"Yes Ma'am." Victor said simply and started on his way as Marie handed him a sealed letter. As Victor sat in the carriage on the way home his curiosity was intrigued. Why

had she handed this letter to him? Was he expelled because fortune had given him the wrong carriage. As he was about to break the seal the carriage stopped before his mother's house. Victor peered out and stepped out of the wagon. Lenore saw him from the window and ran out and down the steps to hold her son.

"Victor. I've missed you darling, but why are you here?" Lenore asked as she hugged her son.

"Mother this note is from Mrs. Kelsey." Victor said as he handed the sealed letter to her.

"What is this? Are you in trouble? Has something happened?" Lenore's fear was running rampant.

"Read it mother. I am going to my room to do my studies." Victor exclaimed as he ran in the house. Lenore opened the letter:

*Dear Ms. Wolf,*

*I am writing to let you know why I am sending your son home, although I am sure he will tell you. There was an incident here at the school where a man was found dead. He was the visiting Lord of Sussex. Please know that Victor did nothing wrong, he merely meant to take them out of the carriage as prompted by our gentleman's class for our maiden ball. The Lord's fiancee however is still alive. Lenore his fiancee shall prove some interest to you. She is the Lady Francis that you were eager for Victor to meet. Victor will remain home with books for home study for a few weeks. After Lady Frances* has recovered or passed on then we will return him to his studies.

Mrs. Marie Kelsey

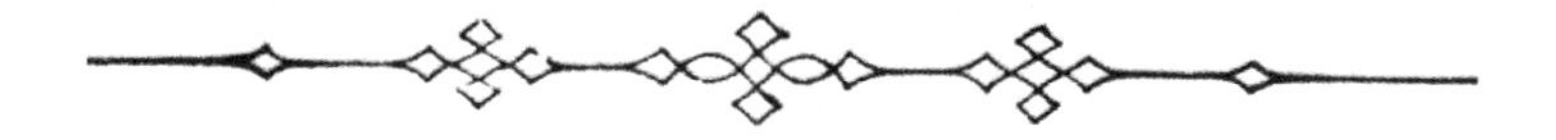

# Chapter 8

After Lenore read the letter she went upstairs to her son's bedroom to be sure he was alright.. He was lying on the floor doing his social studies. He was just learning about President Lincoln and was reading aloud from a newspaper article...

## Proposed Proclamation 95

**On July twenty second year of our Lord 1862 President Abraham Lincoln intended to issue The Emancipation Proclamation by this decree the border state will remain within the Union. However many feel that his proclamation would be more favourable if announced after the civil war ends. Lincoln being an honorable man has**

**decided that this would be in the best interest for our nation.**

Startled by his mother he jumped when she brought him a plate of food.

"Are you alright Victor?" Lenore asked as she looked down at her son. He simply shrugged his shoulders.

"Are you at least hungry?" Lenore offered.

"I guess so. Please leave it I will eat shortly." Victor said as he continued his homework.

"Okay." Lenore said as she walked away. When she got to the kitchen she found another letter placed upon her countertop. She broke the seal and began to read it.

*Lenore,*

*Much time has passed since I have heard from you or about our boy. I am financing this endeavor for our son and would like to know what is going on! I would also like to add that I desire to set aside time in the future to meet my son. It has come to my knowledge that the cottage that I put up for rent years ago has opened again and I want to sell it to you for*

*Victor. I have made all the necessary repairs and everything is now top of the line. I need you to travel to White River so that we may discuss this fully and professionally.*

*Aaron Crawford*

She peeked in on Victor who was deep in slumber. Lenore tried to decide what was best for Victor. She knew the right thing to do but she needed to think. Reading the letter she went up to her room to pack her clothes. She needed space so she had decided to make some supper. They would leave after they had finished eating.

"Mother? Are you ok?" Victor looked at her confused with his eyebrow half cocked after being woken up from a slamming door.

"Yes darling I am fine." Said Lenore as she still held the letter.

"Did you hear that noise mother? What is in your palm?" Asked Victor as he pointed to her hands. Lenore not realizing she still had it looked at her hands.

"Oh it was a late delivery from the post." Said Lenore as she went to put it away and start supper. She needed to finish packing so they could go on the voyage to White River. As Victor followed her it reminded him that none of his clothes were with him.

“Mother not to add to your troubles but I am in desperate need of funds for trousers and shirts again.” Victor said as he thought of his almost empty dresser.
"I will arrange it with the benefactor that you are in need of these funds” Lenore knew it would be hard to explain these extra items to Aaron. But he was obligated to provide these things for their son. After preparing a light supper and sending a servant out to the carriage house they were almost on their way. . The stars were lit in the night sky and a great night for the carriage to have arrived late. They had to bring a few extra blankets. Although it was July the nights could get fairly chilled. Victor went out first and handed the driver the bags. He recognized him from the school but did not say a word. As Lenore walked out Victor did what he was trained to do and helped his mother in first.
“Good job you're doing Master Victor. You’ll be dazzling the ladies before you know it.” Said the driver.
“Thank You Sir.” Said Victor as he boarded the carriage with his mother. He sat down on the opposite side as she then covered with a blanket.
“Do you know that man Victor?” Asked Lenore.
“I know of them mother.” he responded
“That was the driver of the carriage that The Duke of Sussex and Lady Frances rode in.” Victor said as he began to feel unsure of the situation.
“We shall be fine my son and your school will get back to us in no time about the situation.” Lenore said as she placed her hand upon Victors as to comfort him.

# Chapter 9

As the carriage arrived in White River a tall young man about Victor's age helped Lenore out of the carriage. He had brown hair and eyes.
"Good morning Ma'am. My name is Lucas." Said the strange but kind lad.
"Good morning Mr. Lucas." Said Lenore as she proceeded up the walkway. Victor handed over his mother's luggage and stepped out of the carriage immediately.
"Do you think you can handle all of it?" Victor asked.
"Doesn't exactly travel light, does she Victor?" Asked the driver.
"NO Sir she doesn't." Victor chuckled as he handed the driver more bags from the back of the carriage.
"Sir you called me by name. Do I know you?" Asked Victor as he stopped suddenly.
"Yes Sir. I was the driver that…" The driver was stopped mid sentence.
"Victor, do not bother that man, he has a rather large job in front of him." Lenore exclaimed as she came back for her hand bag and handed the driver some coins. He took the coin and nodded as Victor walked up to a cornfield. As the

driver unloaded the rest of the luggage.
"May I ask who you might be again?" Lenore asked.
"I was the driver that drove Lord Susexx and Lady Frances to the school Ma'am." Said the driver.
"And what of them? I know that Lord Susexx has passed. What of his Fiance?" Lenore asked.
"She turned into a beast Ma'am and was shot in the heart." The driver looked mortified at his own explanation.
"OH! Good Lord!" Lenore exasperated.

Meanwhile Victor was exploring the cornfield. At the edge there was a line of trees heading into the woods. The corn stalks were now at least as tall as he was. As he was exploring he lost his footing and almost fell into a ravine that was very steep. He walked around it to see how big it actually was. After seeing how deep the ravine was he had decided he best be on his way back to his mother. Hearing her call he began walking back to the plantation.
"There you are dear. Come. We are going to get a ride from here to the cottage where we will be staying." Explained Lenore as he noticed all their things were on a wagon.
"Mother? A cottage?" Victor argued.
"Yes, a cottage. You need a low profile and this is our best solution." Explained Lenore as she handed him a small suitcase and sat in the front of the wagon as Victor climbed into the back.
"I AM NO ANIMAL TO BE RIDING LIKE THIS." Victor pouted angrily to himself. As the wagon approached the cottage Victor jumped off.
"Mother, I tire of this. I am going exploring." Victor yelled not waiting for an answer. He ran off through the woods taking everything in. Coming to the edge of the woods he saw the tree line from earlier and the cornfield.

Victor conversing with himself.

"Now to go explore that ravine in depth." He knew that he must be efficient because his mother would send the constable after him. Wandering through the cornfield towards the ravine he caught a glimpse of something light blue that looked like it may have been a petticoat. Trying to keep his focus he decides to move closer. The ravine was slippery towards the edge full of uprooted branches. As he looked inward there was a narrow pathway. He followed it curious as to where this adventure would take him. Traveling further down he noticed that the walls had some indentations, almost like shelves and there was a waxy coating on them, a great place to put candles for light. As he came closer to the bottom he could hear water in the distance. The thought of finding a waterfall or even gold was exciting. Victor was very curious and adventurous; but nothing could prepare him for what he was about to see. In front of him was an underground waterfall about five hundred feet tall and at the base was a very wide river that almost touched the other side of the cave. Looking back up he noticed that the sky was still visible.
"A unique place indeed." Said Victor to himself. Wanting to explore and knowing it was getting to be nightfall he continued on. He wanted to get to the base of the waterfall. Victor knew that he was not ready to go back to the cottage. Becoming darker he didn't realize how long he had been exploring and began to vacate the cavern. Upon reaching the top he found that he exited closer to the tree line. He heard laughing and thunder approaching. Looking to the outside edge of the ravine he saw the flash of blue again. Not being able to make out what it was. The thunder clashed and he heard what sounded like a branch snap. He felt someone or something run by him and saw the flash of blue again. He ran, reacting by pulling it by the arm and it almost fell into the deep ravine. The girl panicked and let out a blood curdling scream. Victor realized that what he had saved was a maiden with curly red hair and beautiful blue eyes.

"It's ok! Shhh... She stopped and brought herself back to composure confused. Victor couldn't believe the beauty of the creature before him. Without thinking she was gone. He searched the edge of the woods for her and he finally caught a glimpse of her.
"My apologies, I didn't mean to startle you." Victor said, feeling odd coming from the woods edge. She turned to run again but Victor grabbed her arm to stop her. Getting a closer look at her beauty. Victor dropped his arms feeling as though he may have held on a little too long. The maid was about five foot five. Her long red hair blowing in the wind. Her eyes were red and bloodshot from tears and screaming. She was very enticing. Victor could tell she was staring at him in fear. He decided at that moment his school training would be of much help in this situation. Victor smiled at the lovely maiden.
"Sir you did not startle me I simply tripped over that branch there." The maiden exclaimed.
"Are you sure I didn't startle you?" Victor asked again to reassure himself. She nodded her head and he was sure she was being tenacious.
"Then allow me to introduce myself, I am Victor. Victor Wolf. I must say your eyes are quite lovely. It's as if I'm looking into the ocean." Victor complimented as he bowed and kissed her hand.
"Thank you Victor, My name is Julienna Kelsey. But unfortunately I must leave. I must go and find my sister and my friend." Julienna stated as she turned around looking for them. Victor wanting to leave found his opportunity to get away unnoticed. Running as fast as he could to create as much distance as possible. Victor went home and helped his mother unload. She finally talked to him after much apologizing for taking off.
"I must be more mindful of where I travel" he couldn't get the image of the beautiful maiden with curly red hair out of his head. Victor tries to keep himself busy with settling the house for his mother.

# Chapter 10

Lenore began to get herself settled hoping that it wouldn't be long before they heard from the Academy. Until then she had to do business with Victor's father Aaron and purchase this estate for him. She had received a letter to meet with him and she was preparing to be picked up soon. Victor watched her scramble about.

"Mother where are you going? You've been getting prepared for hours." Said Victor, awaiting an answer.

"I am to meet the owner of this cottage to purchase it for you." Stated Lenore.

"Mother, this is a simple cottage. Why must we live here?" Said Victor as he sighed.

"You will need a place to live when you are not in the Academy." Said Lenore in plain words as she continued to bustle around ignoring her son's blaine disrespect.

"I. Why will I need to live here and where shall you be? Victor gaffed although he had no quarrel living in this area due to a certain red haired maiden. Victor smiled as he thought of the lovely Julienna.

A man with two horses arrived. They beckoned for Lenore to get into the saddle.
"Where's the wagon?" Asked Lenore.
"NO wagon today Ma'am. The Master said you could ride." Smiled the servant. Lenore being ... Lenore was very upset with the man's cruel statement.
"I shall be back within a sennight Victor." Shouted Lenore. Victor waved her off biting an apple. After she was gone Victor threw the apple off into the woods and decided to wander to town. Victor was walking through the corn field a few days later when he saw her again. The girl with those red curls, and he couldn't forget those ocean blue eyes. He had dreamt of her every night since he met her. He longed to see her again.
"Well, hello again. Julienna? Is that correct" Victor asked coyly as he flashed a brilliant smile. Where did she come from? Victor whispered to himself. She flashed a smile at him as her cheeks started to match her hair.
"Victor. I was hoping to see you again. It's not everyday a handsome stranger saves my life." She giggled. Victor couldn't believe this was really happening
"I would like to take you somewhere special." Victor smiled.
"I would love to go." Julienna said happily.
"When? Can you meet me just outside of town? Let's say tomorrow at dusk?" He hesitated thinking of the place he wanted to take her as he smiled and ran his hand through his hair.
"At dusk?" Julienna asked suspiciously.
Victor smiled, glad that he had peaked her interest.
"Yes. Dusk will work fine. We will need to walk to where I want to take you. Do not wear those beautiful gowns that attract me so." Victor smirked and continued.
"You will need good boots and some clothes you won't mind getting...dirty." He blushed.

"Couldn't have that now could we?" Julienna smiled and laughed.
"My mother may murder me if I have a speck of dirt on me especially after just washing this dress." Julienna spun around waving her dress.
"I worry not of a speck of dirt, she may murder both of us if she finds..." Victor trailed off as he touched her face. His eyes were set on hers. He bent down to kiss her but stopped himself. Just inches from her lips holding her hand in his hand.
"Julienna. I really want to kiss you...but I will not."Victor tried to steady his breathing "Not just yet." he whispered, feeling a heat between their bodies.
"I must be going. It's getting late." Julienna hesitated.
"I really must speak with my parents if we are to court.." She said as she pulled his hand down from her face and said goodbye as a lady would.
"Julienna?" Victor started after her. She turned and smiled.
"Tomorrow evening, everything will be amazing." Julienna said, turning to walk away. Victor watched and as soon as she was gone he went into the cornfield to where the gully was.
"Tomorrow night she will be mine." Victor smiled to himself.
After she had gone Victor began the walk home. It was a quiet summer evening with the peepers chirping. After a little while he walked in the front door. It shut loudly.
"Where have you been?" Asked a very angry Lenore.
"I only went for a walk, mother." Victor said louder than he meant to.
"I have been worried for you since I arrived and you were not here." Lenore said back as she crossed her arms over her chest.
"I only went for a walk, mother. It's not like anything happened to me." Stated Victor.

“I will be going to do more negotiations tomorrow and you will stay home!” Shouted Lenore.
“And if I refuse?” Victor challenged her. Lenore walked close to him, her eyes red as she began to speak.
“You will not dare to disobey me again.” She growled. Victor quickly walked to his room and slammed the door. He slammed it hard enough that the birds outside the cottage flew away in a panic. In the morning Lenore rode off again for the negotiations. Victor waited for her to leave. He went about the house and made it his own. Taking down anything that would make it appear a woman had lived there at all. He found a blanket and candles. As late afternoon approached he began walking first to the waterfall cavern and then into town to meet Julienna. When Victor approached town he stood in the shadows. He saw her.
“Julienna?” Victor called to her. She looked around and focused upon Victor.
“I was wrong about those dresses. This is better.” Victor teased. Julienna blushed.
“Shall we?” Victor held out his arm anticipating the events he had planned as he smiled.
“You wouldn't believe the day I have had today. I'll be glad to put it all behind me.” she said, taking his arm.
“Well then let the night begin. So that I may put that beautiful smile back on your face.” Victor stated as they walked arm and arm. Julienna smiled.
“There is that lovely smile I like to see.” Victor put his finger up to her chin. He looked into her eyes much longer than a moment. They began walking toward the outside of town. Victor could feel his palms sweat. He had an urge to stare deep in her eyes like he was looking into her soul. They continued to walk until they came to the cornfield where Victor saved Julienna from falling. They walked through the

corn to a huge cavern. The terrain was muddy and slippery as it went down a steep grade.
"Do you trust me?" Victor asked as he raised his lantern.
"Of course?" Julienna squeaked out.
"That didn't sound too reassuring."said Victor jokingly.
"Do you have a wolf hiding down here to finish off my bad day??" Julienna joked back. Victor not answering right away felt the blood rush to his face. Then he cleared his throat.
"No something far more spectacular." Victor said, trying to reassure her and himself.
They walked deeper into the cavern that felt like it would go on forever. Looking at her eyes enjoying the color of the cave walls bounce off her blue eyes. Victor had lined the wall with candles earlier. Keeping the cave from being totally black. As they got closer to the bottom it started to flatten and they could hear the sound of water. It sounded like a fast flowing river.
"OK. I want you to close your eyes." Victor said.
"What?" it sounded like a whisper over the sound of the water.
"Trust me." Victor whispered into her ear. The water was very loud. She closed her eyes and he tied a piece of fabric around them. The fabric was a silk tie from the school.Taking the lead and warning her off each step making sure she was safe. He needed to get her down to the bottom. Wisping past her he realizes he startled her with his quick movement. He could feel the fog coming up from the end of the cave. It felt as though the fog was making the rocks slippery; he grabbed his whip and cracked it using it to wrap it around a nearby root. Julienna gasps when he let go of one of her hands to get a better grasp. It's a good thing he remembered to grab it or they both would have fallen.

“It's OK. It was just me.” Victor said to calm her already shot nerves. Stopping her abruptly he  pulled her down by her hands.
“I know you can't see anything and today you may have some trust issues, but when I take the blindfold off I want you to keep your eyes closed for a moment longer. OK?” Victor Explained.   She nodded. Victor fumbled with the knot to remove the blindfold from her face.  His heart was pounding in suspense awaiting her reaction as Victor took off the blindfold.
“Open your eyes on the count of three. One, two, three.” Victor whispered into her ear.  She opened her eyes. She took everything in awe.  Looking around at everything. Victor took her hand within his.  VIctor looked at Julienna as she glanced up.  She must have expected to see the ceiling of the cave. Victor thought to himself.
“What a wonderful night!”  Said Victor as Julienna looked into the clear warm night sky with tons of wonderful stars.
“I can never thank you enough for this!” Julienna whispered as she turned to look at him. She squeezed his hand and he squeezed back.
“You don't need to.” Victor whispered in disbelief that he was her with her. Everywhere they turned there was beauty. She looked over at Victor and smiled as he smiled back, without sense she kissed him. Victor was in shock and paused before deepening the kiss.
“I'm sorry. I should not have done that.” Julienna apologized.
“No, I should have.” Victor kisses her again with angest. A deep passion filled both of them until they had to pull away. Victor holding her in his arms not wanting to let her go. Beckoning her to sit with him they watched as the world spun around them. Finally they laid down on the blanket not wanting this night to end.
“However did you find this place?” Julienna asked.

“Next time.” Victor stated. As they lied on the soft blankets. Laying behind her with her in his arms. He held her hand watching her doze off from the sound of the calming waterfall hitting the rocks. Playing with her hair Victor slowly fell asleep.
Awaking to feel the warm sun on him with his eyes closed he felt as though someone was watching him.
“That's kinda creepy. Watching someone sleep like this.” Victor joked as he opened his eyes. Julienna smiled.
“So are you telling me you have not watched me sleep all night?” She asked, giggling.
“No. That's a creepy thing to do. But did you know you talk in your sleep? Quite amusing.” Victor laughed loudly.
“I do not talk in my sleep.” Julienna sat up and laughed.
“It's okay. You were talking about me. I never knew that I was a God.” Victor stated sarcastically.
“Okay you know what? Now you're gonna get it.” Julienna got up and walked toward the river, laughing. Victor was curious as to where she was going.
“Julienna, please be careful it may be weak there.” No sooner did Victor warn her when the cave floor gave way. Victor lunged and managed to grab her arm just in time. Somehow he had managed to pull her to safety. They were both gasping. Victor looked her over.
“Are you alright?? Are you hurt? Is your arm ok?” Julienna interrupted him.
“I'm fine, just my pride is injured. But I told you that you were gonna get wet...” she joked as Victor looked at his shirt. It was soaked but then he noticed Julienna's arm.
“I did hurt you, look at your arm, it's scratched.” Victor exclaimed. Although it was more like a gash.
“I'm fine I could just as easily be dead.” Julienna protested. Victor took a cloth and wrapped her arm. It was bleeding pretty good. She pushed his hands away as it did sting. As

she kept insisting she was ok. Julienna pulled Victor back down to the blanket when he was done torturing her wound. They lied back down on the blanket for a moment longer. They were looking up at the bright sunshine. Catching a glimpse of something in the distance.
"What is that?" She asked Victor as she stretched her arm out straight. Victor looked where she was looking.
"I think we've been spotted. It's time to go." Victor said as he stood up and started to gather his things. Hoping it wasn't the constable or worse...his mother.
"Will we be in..." "Trouble? Probably. But it was worth it to spend time with you." Victor interrupted. He looked up and the person was gone. Then he looked at Julienna.
"Tell me you're going to keep those clothes." Victor laughed as he bent down to kiss her. "And the cold." Julienna giggled.
"Is there an easier way out of here?" Julienna asked.
"No. Same way out. But it will give me more time to pick on you." Victor teased more.
"It will give me a good view if I am following you." Julienna said playfully. After a while they reached what was left of the corn field.
"The farmer must have cut it." Julienna said. Victor was in his own world.
"Do you want to go with me?" Victor asked.
"Go where?? Another surprise?" Julienna asked hopefully.
"Into the woods at my cottage. I don't live within town. I like to be alone. It will be quiet and we will have more time alone." Victor smiled. Julienna smiled back.
"I do not want this to end but I do have to get home." Victor's smile faded. His eyes grew dim.
"Please. I could really use the company today." Victor pleaded.

"I will personally make sure you will not get into any trouble. On my honor." Victor promised.
"How is it I just don't see that happening?" Julienna said as she kissed Victor.

## Back at home

Victor took Julienna's hand and walked her through the familiar trail to his home. It was a winding trail with hills and bumps. You could definitely get lost if you didn't know where you were going. After a while they reached a clearing. There was a small cottage in the back. A few trees around it and some flowers. It was just homey. As they approached the cabin Julienna expected to hear something. Maybe a bird singing or an animal call but it was silent. He walked up and opened the door.
"Please, sit here." Victor said as he pulled out a chair for her. He left the room for a few moments giving her time to study her surroundings. He came back with some supplies.
"I really want to treat that arm of yours. I know it's just a scratch but please let me take care of it." Victor insisted. Julienna put her arm on the table while studying Victor working. He was mixing some power in a bowl. Then he had a very pretty purple flower. She recognized it as wolfsbane. He handled it very cautiously. Victor came over to Julienna and lightly rubbed a flower petal on her arm.
"Does it hurt, burn or ache??" He asked.
"No it doesn't, it stings a little. Are you a healer?" Julienna replied. As Victor put the powder on her arm and bandaged it.
"My Mother showed me how to do this when I was young. I was always reckless." Victor chuckled.
"There, all better." Victor said as he kissed Julienna's hands. Victor knew the look in her eyes said it all.

"Have something to eat and I shall take you home." Letting her get her rest Victor decided to go to the stable and ready his horse. Once at the stable he heard a noise coming from behind him. He Quickly turned to find Julienna behind him; she must have followed him to the stable without him hearing.
"You startled me." Victor said, taking from the stall his horse and putting his saddle on the animal. Setting Julienna in front of himself on the horse and riding to her estate. Everyone was asleep so Victor was able to sneak her in and get out quickly.
Victor rode back off to the cottage barley beating his mother back. He layed in bed pretending to be asleep.
"Why in the world is there wolfbane in my kitchen?!" He heard Lenore shout. Covering his head with the blankets he began to laugh praying that she didn't hear him. Suddenly he heard the door to his room slam open.
"What were you doing with that?" Asked Lenore, as she held up a gloved hand holding the wolfsbane. Victor startled, jumped in bed.
"I thought it was pretty. So I…" Victor rambled looking for the right thing to say.
"I suppose it does not matter. Our business is done and we will be returning home." Exclaimed Lenore. Victor now jumped out of bed.

“No mother.  Not now we can’t!”  Exclaimed Victor as he begged not to leave.
“We will be leaving in the morning.  If you made a friend you may come back a few times on your own, if you can show you are mature enough.”  Said Lenore.  Victor pouted but decided that it wasn’t worth it and went to pack his things willingly.  Lenore also started packing her things as they awaited the carriage to arrive in the morning.

# Chapter 11

***After they arrived home from White River a few days later:***

Victor ran down the stairs to answer the door since his mother was away. He saw a familiar face standing at the threshold.
“Hello Victor.” Said Daniel as he stood next to Rebekah. Not thinking he just wrapped his arms around both of his friends.
“What?... How?” Victor couldn’t find the right words.
“We were granted leave to see you.” Exclaimed Rebekah.
“I can’t believe you are here!” Victor said again.
“Let’s go for a walk.” Suggested Daniel.
“Yes, let's.” Said Rebekah excitedly as she grabbed him by the arm and rushed him off the patio. Running towards the woods surrounding the house. Both smirked as they ran from Daniel. Climbing trees and in the underbrush Rebekah giggled as she hid on Victor. Victor looked up and saw Daniel climbing higher in a pine tree. Then he heard Rebekah and his attention diverted. Wanting to be the one

who caught her, Victor went into tunnel vision to find her, but instead he ran into Daniel.
“Found you Daniel.” Victor yelled. Daniel scuffed and began climbing down the tree. Victor kept hearing Rebekah giggle and was following her voice. Daniel followed as well. A moment later they heard a blood curtailing scream. They ran directly after the sound. They found a huge waterfall and saw Rebekah fall from the top of the waterfall. Victor and Daniel’s eyes got wide as they both ran after her. Daniel jumped as Victor grabbed him and stopped him mid-fall. Daniel, secretly glad that Victor had been there to grab him as he watched Rebekah fall straight into the roaring water beneath. Not able to catch her, they looked at each other while they waited impatiently for her to resurface. After what felt like a fortnight she finally popped to the surface coughing, and struggling for breath. She fought off the current and was able to pull herself to shore. She lied there for what felt like was years. Victor and Daniel began to follow a rather steep path down to Rebekah.
"It's okay Rebekah. Breathe." Coxed Daniel. She wrapped her arms around Daniel as Victor rubbed her back.
“What were you thinking!” Daniel screamed in disbelief of her craziness.
"What happened? Did you slip?" Victor asked thinking that Rebekah lost her ever loving mind.
"I tripped on a rather large root." Coughed Rebekah. Daniel thought for a moment looking at Victor in disbelief.He looked up at the clouds starting to roll in.
“There were no trees at the base of the waterfall.” Explained Victor. They both glanced at each other not believing a word she said.
“Just to see what it was we should take a peek at what you tripped over.” Said Daniel while holding her long wet blond hair back from her face.

"We should go back up when you are ready." Said Victor to Rebekah. Rebekah, still coughing slowly nodded her head. After a while they hiked back up to the top of the waterfall. At the base there were giant stones but no trees were close.
"Where were you when you tripped?" Shouted Victor over the waterfall.
"Over there." Shouted Rebekah back as she pointed. They all walked over that way and were looking down at the ground.
"I don't see anything you could have tripped over." Said Victor holding the hair out of his face.
"What's this?" Asked Daniel as he pulled a large rope. Suddenly they heard stones crashing. The ground shook below them. The waterfall released more water. It was thunderously loud now. Much louder than before as they covered their ears and dropped to their knees. The three looked around at each other now.
"WHAT DID YOU DO?!" Exclaimed Victor as he pulled the rope from Daniel's hands.
"I MERELY PICKED UP THAT ROPE!" Screamed Daniel back. The rumbling and shaking began to slow. The rushing of the waterfall slowed. Rebekah, who noticed a new path while they were yelling at each other, had begun to trail off on her own. Daniel and Victor continued to bicker back and forth placing blame on the cause of the Quake. Daniel's eyes shifted looking from one side to the other to see what had caused the rocks to shift. In looking for the change of terrain he noticed that Rebekah was no longer standing there with her blank stare.
"Where is Rebekah now?" Asked Victor as he raised his hand to Daniel to stop his incessant complaining. Daniel stopped offended and looked around.
"Over there. The quake opened a new path." Said Daniel as he pointed to it. Victor walked over and began to follow

the opening of the cave, seeing Rebekah in the distance she was now at the bottom of the waterfall.
"There appears to be a cave back here." She yelled to them as she walked in.
"Rebekah please wait." Yelled Victor.
"There could be an animal in there." Daniel yelled as he slid on the moss covering the steep limestone pathway.
Rebekah looked around as she was wringing the water from her dress. Daniel was right behind her. Victor entered a moment later. The cave was extravagant. There was light flowing in from a distance.
"What in tarnations were you thinking?" Daniel grabbed Rebekah's arm a bit harder than intended. Rebekah winced as she pulled away out of his grasp.
"I am fine. I am not injured aside from tripping on that darn rope and you're unforgiving grip!" Shouted Rebekah as she shoved him away.
"What if you had been hurt? You did just fall off a waterfall." Daniel argued as he pulled her back to him.
"Obviously I am fine. I am standing right in…" Rebekah's voice trailed off.
All the while Victor was roaming the cave. Something shiny caught his eye. He walked over to see what it was. He gently guided himself along the cave wall. Out of nowhere a sharp pain caught his attention. He realised he had cut his arm on the cave wall. He glanced back at the wall and pulled the object out.
"Hey come look at this." Said Victor as he glinted at it. Daniel and Rebekah had stopped arguing long enough to run over to Victor.
"I think it's a diamond." Said Victor as he held up the stone. Rebekah held her hand out and Victor handed it to her.
"I think you're right." Rebekah stated in awe and then handed it to Daniel.

"If it's a diamond someone has to be aware of it." Daniel explained as he began to look around. Victor was back at the cave wall pulling more stones.
"There's more than diamonds." Exclaimed Rebekah as she brought rubies and emeralds to show Daniel. Victor by now had three solid handfuls of stones in his pockets while Rebekah was also filling hers.
"We need to leave. Something doesn't feel right." Stated Daniel in a hushed tone. He reached over and grabbed Rebekah by the hand. She held his hand and began to follow him towards Victor. Walking past Rebekah touches Victor's shoulder to get his attention. Victor turned.
"I...We will come back to this." Victor groaned in a husky tone. His chocolate eyes glowed with streaks of red in them. Daniel jumped back slipping on the luminous undergrowth.
"What's wrong? Daniel?" Asked Victor. Daniel backed away slowly. Victor started to walk towards him. Backing up faster and realizing he needed to get out of there he turned and grabbed Rebekah by the arm. He pulled her up the pathway frantically screaming.
"What is it!? What is wrong with you?" Rebekah stopped and pulled her aching arm away. Daniel pulled frantically at Rebekah again.
"No we must go NOW! We will talk later but now we must..." Daniel tried to explain as fear had ahold of him. Out of the shadows appeared a wolf. Growling and circling with its teeth bared.
"RUN!" Whispered Daniel to Rebekah. Rebekah's eyes grew large and now fear captured her. Daniel took off like a bolt of lightning leaving Rebekah frozen in fear. The wolf chased after Daniel. Rebekah screamed as something grabbed her hand. Weak from fear she felt as if she would pass out.

"It's just me." Whispered Victor. Rebekah wrapped her arms around him and sobbed. Not too far in the distance they heard Daniel screaming. As they stood up Victor wiped her tears.
"It's nightfall. We know the wolves are out. We need to be as quiet as possible." Holding hands they ran towards Daniel's screams. Victor began to see the reason behind his screams. Victor and Rebekah try to comfort Daniel but laying off to the side was Daniel's bloody arm.
"Help...me.." Daniel whimpered. Victor looked him over in shock that his arm was detached.
"Is it bad?" Asked Daniel with tears stinging his eyes. Rebekah looked to Victor and then to Daniel not knowing what to say.
"If we take him out of here he may not make it." Whispered Victor to Rebekah trying to avoid Daniel hearing him.
"If we leave him he definitely will not make it. He's our friend, how can we do anything else?" Rebekah urged calmly.
Victor looked to Rebekah and noticed she was wearing an apron. He thought for a moment and ripping the apron off of her he used it as a tourniquet to stop the blood flow.
"Grab the other piece over there." Ordered Victor as he pointed it out.
"The other huh...NO! I am not…I refuse"
"Just grab it Rebekah! So he may have a chance at keeping his damn arm!" Victor hollered.
"MY WHAT!!! You mean my arm is.." Daniel panicked as he lifted his good arm.
"OH there it is!" Daniel fainted. Rebekah tied up his nub with the apron while Victor grabbed Daniel's arm and trying to keep the limb alive he wrapped it in what was left of Rebekah's apron with wet leaves knowing that she would not touch it ,he tied it to Daniel's back.

# Chapter 12

***With the change of the season Victor is now back to school.***

“Ready to go to carriage duty?” Daniel asked.
“Which arm are you gonna hold out?” Victor sarcastically pointed to Daniels' damaged apendenge.
“Haha aren’t we comical today. It’s your fault I have this appendage problem.” Replied Daniel as they approached carriage duty.
“I could have cut your air supply off and I’d be dating your girlfriend, but I am not really that cruel.” Stated Victor as his hand reached into the carriage. Coming out of the carriage Rebekah looked at them arguing back and forth.
“I don’t know what either of you are arguing about ,neither of you have my eye.” Stated Rebekah as she giggled. Daniel reached for her hand though she avoided his grasp and helped herself into the carriage. Victor snickered as Daniel pouted. Rebekah looked out the carriage window and blew a kiss towards Daniel. She enjoyed teasing him. At the end of their lesson they had free time. They decided they were hungry so they walked to the kitchen.

“BOY’S how y'all doin? Ready fer some creole?” Jonathan bellowed.
“Creole? What is that?” Asked Daniel looking at Jonathan confused.
“Oh I reckon it be from Louiseana. From the south ren bayou. ‘Most as good as dem dar frog legs.” Jonathan boasted.
“Jonathan do you have any volume softer than LOUD AND OBNOXIOUS?!” Stepped in his wife with her hand over her ears.
“Mr. Kelsey, do you have a banjo?” Asked Victor.
“Do not ask him to play that noise machine!” Exclaimed Marie. Jonathan laughed as he swatted his knee and slopped creole on the kids plates walking by. Victor and Daniel looked at it then at each other.
“Do you think he would actually put frog legs in here?” Asked Victor.
“I wouldn’t trust anything that he made,” Daniel stated. Both boys walked with each other to the trash can and dumped their food plate and all in it. They then went to sit with Rebekah. They watched her put the food in her mouth.
“What?” Rebekah asked dumbfounded chewing on her food.
“I think I saw it move.” Daniel said loudly.
“I think I saw a whole frog in it.” Exclaimed Victor. Rebekah screamed, dumping her food on the boys.
“Well I was hungry ,now you two enjoy cleaning up. Watch out for the frog!” she turned on her heels.
After the rest of the classes blew by Victor had decided to go to bed. But once again he could not sleep. It was another late night. This was beginning to be a pattern. Since Victor couldn’t sleep, he had decided to go for a trip to see Julienna since it is the weekend. He went out to the stable and readyed a horse. He had convinced himself he would only

be gone a few days or so. After a few hours of riding he was getting close and went to the cottage. He tied up his horse and went into town where he ran into Aaron Crawford.
"Hello boy." Said Aaron to Victor.
"Sir?" Victor questioned.
"My son needs an escort for his date tonight. Would you be interested in earning some coin?" Aaron asked him.
"Why would I do that for some pampered brat." Spat Victor.
"What a shame I suppose Miss Julienna will be most disappointed." Aaron guilt tripped him.
"Julienna? Well, I suppose I can sketch time into my schedule." Victor said as he ran his hand across his chin.
"There's a good lad!" Aaron slapped his back and handed him a purse full of gold.
"Be in the carriage in precisely twenty minutes. And comb your hair boy." Aaron explained as he pointed to the carriage. Victor starts to adjust himself, to look presentable. He recognized his son immediately from passing with Lenore. Coming closer to Aaron and presenting himself once he was adjusted. Victor boarded the carriage and he was headed towards home. As the horses led them toward Julienna's house he could hear her and Mary arguing outside as he approached her home. As the carriage came to a stop Victor reached outside and reached for her hand not wanting Mary to see him. Victor helped Julienna into the carriage. As she sat she looked out the window pouting.
"Julienna??" He spoke softly. She frowned until she recognized his voice and looked up at him.
"Victor??" Julienna asked. She reached over and took his hands. She recognized his voice right away.
"I know that you do not want to be here, but you must give Aiden a chance." Victor explained to Julienna. Julienna looked into Victor's eyes. They were so mesmerizing. She found herself lost in the brown mist of his eyes. She shook herself out of it.

“I don’t want Aiden! Victor, I WANT YOU…” Victor stopped her.
“I know my darling. As do I.” Victor confessed. He starred in her deep blue eyes. He found himself dangerously close to her. His hand was on her face. He began kissing her before realizing he was even doing so. She was at a loss for words not knowing what to think. He pulled away as the carriage came to a stop.
“This did not happen Julienna. At least it should not have.” Not giving her a chance to react as he was up and had the door open already for Aiden.
Going back into the carriage and watching them. He saw Aiden kiss Julienna’s hand. Victor's jealousy churning inside.
“Dare he touch my Julienna.” Victor raged imagining the terrible things he could do to him. A deep growl formed in Victor’s throat at Aiden as he reached to fix a stray hair from Julienna's face. Victor saw himself ripping Aiden's arm from the limb.
“Sir...?! Are you going to get the door?” Aiden shouted at Victor. Victor was pulled from his thoughts.
“My apologies Mr. Crawford.” Victor dragged his name out with a scowl.
“Have I done something to offend you Mr...” Aiden said back to him.
“Wolf.” Victor stated.
“Mr. Wolf then?” Aiden spat out.
“Aiden we really should be going.” Julienna interrupted as she grabbed Aiden's hand and pulled him away.
“Yes we shouldn't waste another moment.” Aiden said as he scowled at Victor. Victor ran off to the woods abandoning his duty to host the masquerade.

The next day Victor watched as Julienna was spinning in circles until she had gotten so dizzy that she fell in the tall grass in the field. Julienna laughed. She opened her eyes and tossed her hair behind her. Victor's hand reached out for her.
“You Sir, are going to get us caught.” Julienna exclaimed. Smiling he saw that she had grabbed a big wad of leaves. Helping her up as he caressed her cheek and pulling her face to his. Her smile got bigger as she threw the leaves into his hair. Victor grabbed a handful of leaves himself and chased her when she began running. They threw leaves at each other and neither one of them were very good at the sport. Always missing each other. Victor chased her down again and caught her by her waist misplacing his footing he fell down on top of her in the field. Both laughing and out of breath. Smiling at eachother Victor leaned in to kiss her. She was the one. He knew he needed to be with her.
“Don't tease me. You know we can't.” Julienna said, still wanting to kiss him. Victor ran his hand through her hair. His eyes deep in hers. He kissed her anyways.
“What happened to we can't?” Victor asked.
“I love you Victor. I don't care right now.” Julienna laughed. They sat up on a small hill in the field. Victor had his arms wrapped around her. Breathing in the scent of her hair slowly kissing her neck.
“You are aware that I do not want you courting Aiden my love. I want you for myself. HAve you spoken with your mother?” Victor admitted.
“I know. I did speak to my mother and she has forbidden us to be together.” Julienna grabbed his hand.
“And that arrogant ass Aiden is the best they can come up with for you?” Victor stated.
“He wasn't always this way. We were friends before...” Julienna trailed off remembering how things used to be.
“Do not defend him.” Victor said as he was starting to get angry.

“I'm not defending him, why are you yelling at me Victor?” Julienna yelled at him. Victor took her hand and held it to his cheek kissing it before he lowered it. The hour was before dusk now.
“Julienna, I need to go before it gets much later.” Victor stated as he pulled away.
“No please...I...I want to be with you Victor. Please...don't leave me.” She begged as she pulled on his arm.
“If I don't leave...I might do something we'll both regret. ” Victor said as he released her hand. Grabbing her by the waist pulling her closer. He softly pulled his face to hers and kissed her. Victor could see the tears welling in her eyes.Wiping one of her tears he kissed her again.
“I suppose I must be off to meet Aiden for tea.” Julienna said as she looked off into the distance.
“I will see you soon.” Victor said as he slowly pulled away and left. As Victor stood in the shadows he watched her leave. Growing jealous he started to fill with anger not realizing it he began to phase into a wolf with glowing red eyes. Seeing Aiden he began to chase him and Julienna not knowing what he was doing. Fighting with the beast inside him he wrestled, trying desperately to gain control of himself again. He ran back into the woods after they had gotten away. Victor, still in wolf form laid to rest and fell asleep outside the cottage. When he awoke he was in the form of a man and was also without his knickers. He opened the door to his house and washed and dressed. What in the world happened? He thought to himself. Instead of leaving as he was going to the night before, he was going to run into town to check on Julienna. While doing so she accidentally ran into him. They were in the woods and they had both ran to each other as he had noticed that she had tears coming from her eyes. She threw her arms around him desperate for his embrace.
“What's wrong? What has happened?” Victor asked, worried.
“A creature! It was chasing us just as you left. I was terrified and yet I felt as if you were with me.” Julienna explained seriously.

“Do you know what it was?” Victor asked hoarsely.
“I'm not sure... I...a wolf perhaps? I am so relieved no harm came to you.” Julienna expressed as she embraced Victor.
“I'm not alright Julienna. The wo...creature went after you! A wolf you say?” Victor stated. He had started pacing.
“I do not believe it was a wolf my love.” Victor educated Julienna.
“Well I suppose if they are hungry enough a young girl with long curly red hair would be an enticing snack.” Julienna giggled at her joke.
“Do not say such things. I can't imagine this world without you.” Victor scolded as they began to walk.
“Do you not have to be with Aiden today?” Victor scoffed.
“Are you trying to get rid of me Victor?” Julienna half joked.
“No. Of course not.” Victor cleared his throat.
“I have only one thing to do today, It's important so I must go.” He stated as he looked off into the distance.
“If you must go then I suppose.” She whined to Victor. She didn't want him to leave but she knew there was no point in trying to beg him to stay.
“Interesting, perhaps I shall go search the woods myself for the beast.” Victor exclaimed.
“Perhaps I shall go with…” Julienna tried to explain.
“No my love, it's far too dangerous.” Victor stated as his annoyance was growing.
“What shall I do with myself? Adien is off hunting the beast and I do not want to go home.” Julienna mumbled to herself.
“Absolutely not. That thing is attracted to you. No need to go stir up trouble.” Victor insisted as he pulled her to him. He put his head to hers as he looked into her deep blue eyes.
“Stay here.” Victor commanded.

## ~The Dark Place~

Victor was in the silver mine beneath his house with his mother and an unconscious and bleeding Julienna.

"How did she come to be in my home?" Victor exclaimed, confused.
"I heard a crash and went to check. It was only then I saw her." Lenore exclaimed.
"This is not the right time. The crest is upon us." Victor exclaimed as he was pacing.
"If the townsfolk hadn't killed that beast..." Lenore exclaimed. Victor stood over Julienna as she sobbed in silence and reached for the back of her head.trying to move her leg as she gasped in pain. She started to open her eyes.
"I told you to stay put!" Victor stated angrily to Julienna as he bent down to address her wound.
"You said you had to do something else. So I went for a walk." Julienna grimsed as Victor bandaged her leg and stifled a smile.
"I feel you have met your match Victor." Lenore chimed in.
"It's the red hair. Causes moments of stubborness." Julienna said sarcastically as she gasped while Victor attempted to brace her leg.
"Hush now. You need your rest, nap child." Lenore stated. Laying on the mattress on the floor she grabbed her blanket and closed her eyes. Letting sleep take her over.
Victor was applying the medication to Julienna's head and leg as she slept.
"Mother, I never should have brought her into my life." Victor sadly admitted as he knelt next to her, holding her hand.
"My son you can't help it. Love is not an emotion you can control." Lenore put her hand on Victor's shoulder.
"I should have known better...after all I almost lost her to the river." Victor looked around. He could hear the river still flowing in another section of the cave.
"She is safe for now. Right now we need to find out about those gunshots. Who else was around?" She questioned..

“I have no idea. I was just walking from these caves looking for you, when I heard her screaming. That damn bear…!” Victor stated frustrated trying to hide his secret.
“Here...Why were you looking for me here?” His mother asked.
“You sent me a letter saying you would be here.” Victor responded as he pulled out the letter.

*My dearest Victor,*

*The harvest moon is upon us we must prepare for the feast. There is much to be done in so little time. Please meet me at the river caves where I have stayed in the past for our festivities. It has been a year and I would be much pleased to hear of this Julienna. Do not forget to meet me, my son.*

*Always your mother,*
*Lenore*

“Silly boy. I did not send this. Where did you receive this?” Lenore asked.
“At my cottage. The way I receive all your letters.” Victor said as he puzzled.
“Someone is watching you. You must be careful.” Lenore urged caution.
Victor stood and began to pace. He worried for his secret, his mother and for the woman he loves. Lenore walked up to him. She embraced her son.
“Worrying and pacing will not help. You act of your father. Always worry and dread.” We need to investigate further. As

of this moment, be sure the bear is gone and get the girl to safety." Lenore said matter of factly.

Victor pondered as he remembered the incident. He wondered why the bear was there? There were so many questions left unanswered. Julienna was knocked unconscious by a jack-o-lantern... but he never put one out! Victor knew not to draw attention to himself.
"Is there any reason someone would want you from your home?" asked Lenore.
"No one knows I live there except you, and Julienna." stated Victor. He was becoming annoyed thinking about it.
"And no one hunts near the cottage …?" Lenore asked questionly.
"Mother, I live in solidarity for a reason." Victor was annoyed with the accusation that his mother threw at him.
"That bear must be being hunted. Don't you agree?" Lenore was now grasping at possibilities.
Victor was now more annoyed than ever. His love was lying on a cold cave floor. He needed to get her somewhere safe. His mother was now grasping at straws. She didn't write the letter but someone wants him from his home. They got their way, because now here he was not in his warm house visiting with his mother and instead watching his love bleed everywhere. He feared she would freeze to death. Victor sat back down next to Julienna. Taking off his undershirt in an attempt to keep her warm. His mother standing on the far side of the cave rambling about him being careful. He gently moved her hair from her face.
"...and the purpose for the hole in your home now. Someone knows of the connection." Lenore accused.
"No more mother! No one knows of me or you or anything!" Victor stood shouting at his mother. His brown eyes now had the blood streaks in them.
"VICTOR AARON WOLF! You will not RAISE YOUR VOICE to me!" Lenore punished her son.
"Mother I need to take her...somewhere. My home is not safe now and there is no way I will bring her to her mother or to Aiden this w...AIDEN" Victor realised both stunned and amused.
"Why would your broth.. He be after you?" Lenore asked.

“Julienna, wait what ,brother…? WHAT do you mean! Victor exclaimed. Victor did not have the energy for this conversation. He needed to get Julienna to safety and warmth.
“A lecture for another time mother. I must get her out of here.”  Victor was now exhausted as his thoughts overpowered him.
Victor picked up Julienna and ran out of the cave.

# Chapter 13

The snow was sticking to the ground now and Victor always seemed to be hot even with no covers on him. As he layed in bed the sheets were sticking to him. Although tired he just could not sleep. He kept tossing and turning. He could not get comfortable. He felt restless and tried to find something to put him to sleep. Feeling the urge to get air, he got up and went to the window. Another full moon. He was growing sick of seeing it. He looked over to Daniel snoring with his messed up arm sticking up in the air; he suddenly grew jealous. He could deal with having Daniels arm if he could only sleep at night. Just then he felt something hit his back. He turned to see Rebekah. She motioned for him to come down. Victor threw on some trousers and a shirt and went down to meet her.

"Can't sleep?" She asked when he got to her. Victor was tired but restless.

"Is that all you wanted Rebekah?" Victor said, agitated.

"No. I wondered if, since you're awake if you'll go for a walk with me?" Rebekah asked shyly.

"I suppose we can, since I'm awake." Victor said.
"Won't you want your shoes and some warmer clothes?" Pointed out Rebekah. Victor looked about himself and just shrugged his shoulders.
"I will get my shoes but I am actually quite comfortable." Said Victor as he ran up to grab his shoes.
"Where do you want to go?" Asked Victor as he draped his coat over her shoulders.
"Let's go back to the cave and see if there are any more jewels." Rebekah suggested.
"Why after everything we went through would you want to go back there?" Victor asked hestitley.
"I found an emerald and want one more." Rebekah exclaimed as she showed him the gem.
"All of this for an emerald?" Stated Victor as he rolled his eyes.
"It's for my sister Anna. I want to make her a pair of earrings." Explained Rebekah.
"What of your sister Anna is as spoiled as you? If so I DO NOT want to meet her." Stated Victor still agitated as they headed out. The walk was fast towards his mother's house. They could hear the waterfall rushing in the distance. Rebekah still shivered weather from excitement or the cold Victor wasn't sure.
"We need to take a different pathway with all of the snow." Victor suggested.
"What about that path over there?" Rebekah pointed to a clear pathway within the snow.
"Well isn't that convenient." Victor said smugly. As he looked down at Rebekah. They followed the path that did indeed lead them right to the waterfall. It wasn't as loud as before but it hadn't frozen yet either.
"Be careful of the wet spots and ice. No slipping on anything this time." Joked Victor as he helped her into the cave. The

candle lit up the cave just enough. They walked through until Rebekah found the perfect emerald.
“Hurry up. It's getting cold down here.” Victor complained.
“You are the one that said you were comfortable.” Stated Rebekah matter of factly. Victor not ready to argue, let her have that one.
“Help me with this will you?” Rebekah pleaded. Victor picked up a rock and started to chip away at the limestone. As it became apparent the emerald did not want to come out. Victor’s temper was starting to show. He hit the limestone a bit harder and the emerald fell out onto the floor. He picked it up and handed it to her.
“Thank you Victor.” Said Rebekah as she took it from him. As she held the emerald looking into his eyes he bent over and kissed her softly on the lips.
“No, I’m sorry we can’t do that.” Said Rebekah as she pulled away.
“You’re right we can’t. I’m sorry too.” Said Victor sadly.
“It’s Daniel. I care about him.” Said Rebekah openly.
“You’re both my friends. I won’t ruin that.” Victor said as he handed her another jewel.
“I love it.” Rebekah looked at a heart shaped ruby.
“Then why do I feel so hurt?” Victor said sadly as he ran his fingers through her blond hair.
“It's simple really. You're in love with me.” Explained Rebekah.
“I can’t be in love with you. I’m in love with someone else.” With that being said Victor had decided that there was no way that he was in love with her.
"Best be going Rebekah." Victor said as they headed out. Rebekah followed him as he remembered his manors and helped her out first. They made the short cold walk back to the school. He walked her back to her side of the school.
"Goodnight Victor. Thank you for taking me." Rebekah said.

"You're welcome." Said Victor still sulking. Rebekah turned to make her way in.
"Rebekah! What if I hadn't been up? You wouldn't have gone on your own? Would you?" Victor asked as he leaned on the banister.
"I was gonna wake you or Daniel up by throwing pebbles at your windows. It worked for Uncle Jonathan." She said bluntly. She walked back over to Victor and wrapped her arms around him. Victor hugged back so it wouldn't get any weirder than it already was. This time Victor turned to walk away.
"Victor...!" Rebekah yelled to him. He turned to look and Rebekah jumped into his arms and kissed him. You have to stop this! His mind kept screaming at him but he couldn't. Daniel heard Rebekah yell and went to the open window to see what was going on. He saw Rebekah run into Victor's arms and kiss him. He was kissing her back. It was snowing and they were hardly wearing clothes. Daniel out of anger slammed the window down and broke it. The sound of breaking glass jarred the two apart.
"No this can't happen again!" Victor exclaimed as he gently pushed her back.
"I understand." Stated Rebekah as she handed the ruby back to him.
"It's yours. Make a pendant out of it." Victor said as he handed it back. She nodded and went back to her room. Victor walked back to his room. He never would have told her but he was actually freezing now. He saw Daniel still laying in bed asleep. He layed in his bed with his covers over him and finally fell asleep. The next morning when he had woken up he found Daniel sitting on the edge of his bed.
“Did you have fun last night?” Daniel asked snidely as he was reading Shakespeare’s A midsummer night's dream.

“What are you talking about?” Victor asked as he was rubbing the sleep out of his eyes. Daniel bolted up and threw his book across the room

“DO NOT THINK ME A FOOL VICTOR! I SAW YOU! BOTH OF YOU!” Daniel screamed at him as he yanked the blankets off him. Victor, still not sure what was going on bolted out of bed.

“I DON’T KNOW WHAT YOUR GOING ON ABOUT!” Shouted Victor at Daniel as he pushed him out of his face.

“Rebekah! I saw the two of you last night!” Daniel said in his normal tone as he approached Victor again. Victor shook his head in disbelief.

“That was an accident. It shouldn’t have happened.” Victor admitted.

“But it did. How could you? You knew that…” Daniel’s voice trailed off.

“It just happened, I know you have feelings for her and that's why I told her that I don’t want this.” Victor said as he hung his head in shame.

“How far did it go?” Asked Daniel.

“You saw it. You said so yourself.” Said Victor not wanting to tell him about the first kiss.

“You were both half dressed.” Daniel said again as he walked over and picked up the book.

“It was hot last night and I didn’t want to wear any hot clothes.” Victor said.

“Don’t insult me. I am far from stupid. Did she give herself to you?” Daniel hesitated but was straight forward.

“No. We only kissed and like I said it was a mistake.” Victor said apologetically.

“Victor...? You were hot?” Daniel laughed at him.

“Yes I felt like I was on a spit.” Victor laughed back as he slapped his good arm.

"So where were her clothes?" Asked Daniel as he grabbed his arm.
"Wet. We went for a walk in the snow." Admitted Victor.
"Why are you being so forthcoming? Are you lying to me?" Questioned Daniel.
"I have no reason to lie." Admitted Victor as he lied back down on his bed arms behind his head.
"And if I ask her?" He questioned again.
"I don't know what she will say." Victor said as he sat up on his elbow.
"Breakfast then?" Daniel said as he picked up a pair of trousers and threw them to Victor. Victor caught them and threw them on. He felt as though he was under a scope with nowhere to turn. Daniel was dressed and out the door. Victor was still dressing when he heard the door open again.
"I'm coming Daniel. Let me get my boots on." He said trying to hop on one foot and eventually falling onto his back.
"What have you gotten yourself into my son" Questioned Lenore.
"Mother? What are you doing here." Victor asked, shocked to see her.
"You have certainly made a mess of all my plans for you." Stated Lenore as she helped her son stand up.
"What do you mean mother?" He questioned as he threw on his shirt and began tucking it in.
"I saw you and the girl last night. Apparently I was not the only one to see you both." Explained Lenore.
"Where did you see us?" Asked Victor hoping it was the same place that Daniel saw them.
"In the cave. Kissing that girl." Said Lenore as she paced about the tragedy of a bedroom.
"Then you know that we said it was a mistake." He said.
"Yes I do. But YOU kissed HER. It wasn't the other way around." Lenore chuckled as he was trying to fool her.

Victor was finished dressing and now sitting on his bed with his head in his hands.
"What do you want of me?" Victor asked looking up at her briefly.
"Give her this potion. It will make her forget you." Lenore said as she handed him a small glass bottle.
"What am I to do with this?" Victor said as he shook the bottle lightly.
"Place a drop or two in her drink and she will forget the last couple nights." Explained Lenore.
"What's in it." Asked Victor as he was trying to open it.
"Be careful not to get any on you. There is wolfsbane in it and you are allergic" Exclaimed Lenore as she reached for the bottle.
"Wolfsbane? What will happen if more than a few drops gets in her drink." Asked Victor.
"Nothing but try not to use too much." Explained Lenore as she walked out the door. Victor put the bottle in his pocket, combed his hair and went to breakfast.
"What do you mean nothing happened?" Asked Daniel as he tried not to yell.
"I mean nothing happened. If you're so worried about it then ask Victor." Rebekah lied.
"Victor told me. I just want to hear it from you." Said Daniel roughly as he punched the table. Victor came up behind them and gently touched Rebekah's back to let her know he was there.
"It's okay he knows about last night." Said Victor as he winked at her. Rebekah got up and walked to another table as Victor followed her.
"He doesn't know about the cave." Whispered Victor to Rebekah as he handed her a bowl of oatmeal.
"I'm not hungry." Exclaimed Rebekah as she pushed it away.

"Eat something, please." Victor asked. By this point Daniel was at the table with his breakfast still demanding an answer.
"She will talk when she's ready. Don't be an ass." Said Victor sternly as he pushed Daniel's bowl away.
"Go talk to him. He is not angry with you. He is angry with me." Said Victor as he coaxed her away. Rebekah stood up and looked at Daniel.
"You wanna talk. Let's talk!" Exclaimed Rebekah and she pulled him away with her. After Victor was sure they were gone he took the bottle out of his pocket. He fidgeted with the cork with both bowls in front of him. His fingers were slippery as he was nervous. The bottle dropped out of his hand. Some of it spilled into the bowl. The other bowl he put two drops into. Victor sat down and was eating his oatmail. Daniel and Rebekah came back over laughing and sat down to eat their now cold oatmeal.
"Here you are Rebekah. Eat." Rebekah grabbed her spoon and accidentally grabbed the wrong bowl. Victor saw her and purposely knocked it out of her hands and into Daniels.
"Sorry Daniel I put maple syrup in that one. I thought you said you were allergic, Rebekah." Said Victor as he handed the other bowl to her.
"I am. Thank you for remembering." Said Rebekah as she took the bowl from Victor. They all ate their breakfast and were joking and laughing like nothing happened.
"I'm getting tired." Said Rebekah after half the day had passed.
"Then go to bed." Said Daniel as he was running circles around everyone.
"What's going on with you?" Asked Victor to Daniel.
"I do not know. But I am going for a run around the school grounds." Exclaimed Daniel as he ran off. Rebekah leaned into Victor as she began to doze off.

“Oh no, none of that. Wait until you get to your room.” Said Victor as he caught Rebekah mid-fall and carried her the rest of the way to her bedroom. He laid her down and covered her up.

“I wish I could forget the memories as well.” Said Victor to himself as a single tear dropped from his eye. Then he had another thought.

“How allergic am I? Just a couple drops right.” Thought Victor to himself again. He walked to his room and sat on the bed. He took the bottle out of his pocket and opened it. It had a drop in it. He opened it and let the drop fall onto his tongue. It instantly burned but it was bearable. He then laid down and fell asleep.

# Chapter 14

Victor woke up laying in bed the sheets sticking to him. It was cold outside. Feeling the urge to get air he got up and went to the window. Another full moon. He felt the strangest feeling of deja vu. He looked over to Daniel. He appeared to be asleep but he wasn't snoring now. He walked over and shook him. He didn't respond.
"Daniel!" Victor exclaimed. Victor shook him again. Then he heard tapping on the window. Still shaking Daniel he began to panic. Then the window broke. He turned to see the broken glass on the floor.
"For the love of GOD. Daniel, wake up!" Screamed Victor as he was now punching his chest. Then there came a loud bang on the door. Victor jumped as the door flew open and in burst Rebekah.
"Is everything all right?" She said ,at the scene unfolding in front of her.
"No. He will not respond to me. I think that he is dead!" Victor exclaimed as he began sobbing. Rebekah looked over to Daniel then back to Victor.

“I’m going to go get some help.” She said as she brushed Victor’s hair out of his face then turned and ran out the door. After a few moments a half dressed Jonathan appeared at the door with a very stunned Marie.
“Take him from here Marie.” Said Jonathan in his not so loud boisterous voice. Marie walked over and lowered herself to see his face.
“Come with me Victor.” Marie looked into his eyes as his tears poured from them. She reached out for his hands. As he took them he slowly stood up and walked out with her. Jonathan then looked over at Daniel to be sure that he was indeed deceased. Daniel made no movements, no breathing,nothing. Rebekah returned with the school nurse.
“Rebekah, I sent Victor with your aunt. I want you to take a buggy to his mother. I want her here, NOW!” Jonathan exclaimed. Rebekah nodded and ran off to get Marie.

***Meanwhile in another room:***

“Victor what happened?” Asked Marie as she handed him a cup of tea. Victor said nothing and set the tea on the table as he slouched back into the chair and began silently crying again.
Marie sat next to him and she held his hand. Victor looked down at it and then at her.
“He was my friend!” Victor exclaimed as he pushed her hand away.

"I know he was. I saw your smiles." Marie recalled as she smiled at him. Victor managed a small smile as he wiped away a tear.
"I thought, I thought he was sleeping." Explained Victor as he recalled the past moments.
"Tell me what you remember." Urged Marie.
"I thought he was sleeping. I called out to him many times but he wouldn't stir." Victor slowly shook his head as he turned and looked at Marie. His chocolate brown eyes now streaked with red. Marie had seen this before and recognized it.
"What happened before you went to bed." Asked Marie.
"Carriage duty.. I think? It's foggy." Questioned Victor to his own statement. Marie took a sip of her tea and looking up from it saw Victor sipping his own.
"Do you know what today's date is Victor?" Asked Marie.
"September 22, 1862. Well the 23rd now." Victor said as he wondered why she asked him for the date.
"Victor it's January 3, 1863. President Lincoln just signed the Emancipation Proclamation into effect two days ago." Stated Marie. Victor looked at her and started to laugh.
"That was a good one Mrs. Kelsey. You almost had me. He just suggested that bill yesterday." Victor laughed even harder.
"Come. Look at this." Said Marie, not amused in his laughter, walked over to the window and opened the curtain. Victor walked over and looked out the window. Snow in September.
"You've gone to some great lengths on this one Mrs. K." Said Victor as he backed up from the window. Looking around him, there was still a Christmas garland and ornaments hanging about.
"Is Daniel in on this? Are you ALL playing a huge gag on me?" Exclaimed Victor as he was outright laughing

hysterically with tears rolling down his face. Pulling at his hair. Lenore walked in at that moment.
" Mama I've gone completely mad." He screamed, still laughing and tugging at his hair. Lenore looked at Marie as Marie looked at her.
"I'll take him home for a few days Marie." Stated Lenore as she began to walk her son out. Victor was non-stop babbling now.
"Lenore! I know what he is and what has happened." Stated Marie. Lenore walked up to Marie.
"And what is that?" Said Lenoire more as a threat.
"A wolf. I find out that he killed that boy and is now in transformation ,I'll..." Marie threatened.
"You will what?!" Exclaimed Lenore as her eyes now glowed bright red as she began to growl.
"I'll turn you over to the constable!" Exclaimed Marie. As Lenore was gradually cornering her.
"Let us leave Victor. We will discuss what happened at home." Shouted Lenore as she turned and began walking to the carriage.
After arriving home Lenore dragged Victor into the house he was dead weight. Struggling to get him out of the carriage she pulled him by his trousers not knowing how else to move him. He had finally stopped laughing but was now playing in the snow.
"You need to get yourself up and get inside Victor. You are acting like a fool." Lenore yells.
Ignoring her he jumps into the snowbank while wearing nothing but his trousers Victor lies in the snow and begins moving his arms and legs to form a snow angel.
"Enough! Get into the house now!" Barked Lenore as she growled at him. Victor bolted up and ran into the house but not before he threw a snowball at his mother's head. Victor

laughed as he ran up to his room and fell face first into his bed. Within minutes he was sound asleep and snoring.

"Help me with this will you?" Rebekah pleaded. Victor picked up a rock and started to chip away at the limestone. As it became apparent it did not want to come out Victor's temper was starting to show. He hit the limestone a bit harder and the emerald fell out onto the floor. He picked it up and handed it to her.
"Thank you Victor." Said Rebekah as she took it from him. As she held the emerald looking into his eyes he bent over and kissed her softly on the lips. When Victor awoke from the dream,
He heard banging pots and pans and smelled the most God awful smell. His head hurt from whatever had happened the night before.
"What is that God awful smell?" Victor turned to Lenore who seemed to be making breakfast
"Quail eggs" Lenore responded
"Gross! What happened last night? My head feels like I was run over by a carriage." Victor asked as he rubbed what felt like a knot on his head.
"You drank something that I told you not to touch let alone ingest." Said his mother as she placed a bowl of oatmeal with the quail eggs atop of it in front of Victor. He began eating it even though the smell was throwing it off.
-Flashback begins-
All of a sudden a bottle dropped out of his hand. Some of it spilled into the bowl. The other bowl he put two drops into. Rebekah and Daniel took their bowls from Victor. They all ate their breakfast and were joking and laughing.
"I wish I could forget the memories as well." Said Victor to himself as a single tear dropped from his eye.

“Yes I do. But YOU kissed HER. It wasn’t the other way around.” Lenore chuckled.
“DO NOT THINK ME A FOOL VICTOR! I SAW YOU! BOTH OF YOU!” Daniel screamed at him as he yanked the blankets off him.
"Place a drop or two in her drink and she will forget the last couple nights." Explained Lenore.
"What's in it." Asked Victor as he was trying to open it.
"Be careful not to get any on you, you're allergic" Exclaimed Lenore.
“He will not respond to me. I think that he is dead!" Victor exclaimed as he began sobbing. Victor jumped up from the table. The room was spinning or was it just his head. Pans falling to the floor and clattering along with his breakfast falling to the floor. Victor caught his balance on the countertop and was able to focus on the images in front of him.
“You made me kill him.” He whispered to Lenore.
“NO Victor. I told you to alter her memories. I did not tell you to poison Daniel.” Said Lenore as she was cleaning up the kitchen.
“What is wrong with me?” Asked Victor as he started to help her pick up. Lenore pulled out the kitchen chair and motioned for Victor to join her.
“How does your head feel?” Asked Lenore.
“Like I had an ordeal between a bear mauling me and a tree swing taking me in circles.” Admitted Victor as he held his head.
“The quail eggs and other ingredients were a short term memory recovery for you my son.” Explained Lenore.
“Are you a witch Mother?” Victor questioned as he raised an eyebrow.
“No Victor I am no witch.” Lenore said as she chuckled.

“If you knew that would affect my memory why leave everything out?” Victor asked, looking about the mess.
“I did not expect your reaction. I thought you would just sit there.” Admitted Lenore.
“Why give them back at all? You knew what happened. I did not want them.” Said Victor in a pained tone.
“You need them back to *‘control the beast within’* Victor.” Lenore said as she Aaron’s pocket watch in front of Victor.
“What are you…” Victor trailed off as he picked up his watch.
“We have much to discuss.” Explained Lenore.

# Chapter 15

"Please, I need to see her!" Pleaded Victor to Jonathan.
"She be as hurt as you is ,Victor. She be grieving too." Said Jonathan as he moved blankets and clothes about the market.
"I can't even go back to the school because Mrs. Kelsey had me deemed a threat!" Exclaimed Victor as he took the clothes Jonathan was shuffling around out of his hands. Jonathan looked up at Victor.
"It kills me to see the two of ya go through this. Marie will boil me in me own gumbo if I let you anywhere near me niece!" Explained Jonathan as he pulled the clothes back and placed them down.
"It can be anywhere. A note! I will write her a letter, please just give it to her." Begged Victor. Jonathan scuffed and shook his head. He went around the back and came back with parchment and ink.
"If this backfires on me boy!!!!" Jonathan threatened.
"IT WON'T, I SWEAR!" Exclaimed Victor excitedly as he took the parchment and ink from him and took to a nearby table.

*Rebekah,*

*I am at a loss for OUR grieving. I feel both of your presences and miss you both dearly. These last couple months have been horrid without you my friend. I wish to see you. Within your jewels you carry a heart shaped ruby. Meet me at the cave beneath the waterfall tonight.*

*Victor Wolf.*

Without hesitation Victor folded up the letter and handed it to Jonathan. Jonathan took the letter and placed it in his satchel.
"I make no promises Victor." Said Jonathan.
"I understand Sir." Said Victor as he bowed to his old professor and left.
"At least the boy kept his manors." Jonathan stated as he watched Victor leave.
When Victor arrived home a carriage was pulling away with Lenore standing outside watching it leave.
"Who was that mother?" Asked Victor as he stood next to her.
"It does not matter my son." Said Lenore as she rolled a parchment in her hands and turned to go into the house.

"Why was I to be home so early?" Victor asked as they walked back into the house. Lenore sat on the sofa as Victor sat next to her.
"You are part werewolf and until you can control your morphing I want you in before the moon crests." Explained Lenore.
"The full moon is a few nights away mother." Pouted Victor.
"Yes I am aware but as I said you are new to your phasing and your mind invasion, so I wish you to be home before dark. Understood?." Stated Lenore.
"I do not agree but I understand." Agreed Victor as he slumped back on the sofa arms folded.
"Now a lesson. I have acquired a home for you. Bought it in fact and titled it in your name." Said Lenore proudly as she opened the parchment and showed him the title. Victor took the parchment and read it.
"Mother this home is in South Dakota." Explained Victor.
"Yes actually. White River South Dakota. We lived there before." Said Lenore as she smiled.
"Why do you want me to leave?" Victor asked, upset.
"It's to be safe until you can control yourself." Stated Lenore again.
"And what of funds to live? I know no trade and this woman you wanted me to meet has never shown." Explained Victor.
"The funds are no issue. As I said I bought your home for you out right. There is a silver mine on the property. Inconvenient as it is but you may hire workers." Suggested Lenor. Victor again rolled his eyes and got up to leave.
"Are we done here?" Asked Victor as he took the deed.
"For now. Do not make plans for tomorrow for it will be a long day indeed." Said Lenore as she walked to the kitchen.
Victor went up to his room and dressed for a chilly night. After Victor was sure his mother was asleep he left the house holding a lit candle. He walked the familiar trail to the

waterfall. A smile crossed his face as he thought of finally seeing his friend again. The ground was saturated due to all the snow melting and the waterfall was fast as was the river. He took an umbrella with him as well and as he approached the falls he opened it so as to not get soaked.

# Chapter 16

Victor held the lit candle as he went behind the waterfall. He saw a figure within the dark there.
"WHO ARE YOU? SHOW YOURSELF." Commanded Victor as he shined the light towards the shadow.
"What are you doing here Victor?" Asked Lenore as she drew closer.
"I thought you were asleep."" said Victor, confused.
"I am not. Why are you down here?" Lenore asked again.
"To tell my friend goodbye." Said Victor sadley.
"Then I suggest you hurry time is of the essence." Stated Lenore as she went through the back of the cave and disappeared. Rebekah arrived a few moments later.
"Rebekah. I'm sorry for what I, well I mean…" Victor tried to explain.
"I know it was an accident. It was not your fault." Said Rebekah as she hushed him pushing her fingers to his lips.
"But it was...Rebekah I am leaving in the morning and won't be back. I have been expelled and my mother bought a house for me." Victor explained quickly.
"Leaving? Where?" Rebekah asked.

"I can't say." Said Victor as he lowered his head in shame.
"I am leaving as well. Daniel was my courter and now he's dead." Said Rebekah sadley.
"I really am so sorry." Explained Victor.
"Well I may still marry for love. In my hometown of White River my mother and father have told me I am to marry my sister's childhood friend Aiden." Smiled Rebekah.
"White River?" Victor asked.
"Yes. Just over the border in South Dakota." Rebekah explained.
"Did you remember the ruby pendant?" Asked Victor as he pulled a gold chain out of his pocket.
"Yes I did." Rebakah said as she took out the pendant with a silver clasp on it. She put the chain on it and Victor put it on her neck.
"This is goodbye for now my friend." Said Rebekah as she hugged her friend. The slider on the pendant burnt Victor a little but the pain was tolerable.
"Look me up if ever you are in White River." Stated Rebekah.
"I will." Promised Victor as he already knew he would see her again.

# Chapter 17

As Victor awaited the carriage to go back to White River he thought about all the fine memories he had with his friends and how much he was going to miss them. He laughed out loud when he thought about Jonathan Kelsey and his loud boisterous laugh. A man like him was one in a million. Before long the carriage arrived. Victor boarded the carriage as the driver took his bags.

"Where to Sir?" Asked the driver.

"White River driver." Said Victor as he looked off at his mother's house.

"White River it is Sir." Said the driver as he whipped the horses and they began their journey. The carriage had to take a few detours due to flooding since some snow was beginning to thaw. The few times he went to White River was specifically to see Julienna. A date here and a date there. As Victor finally got to his cabin he noticed the wall was fixed and there was an addition with a new window. The driver dropped off his luggage and left. All Victor could think of now was to find Julienna.

The snow was much more abundant here. There was no way even if he did get a horse from his father, that the horse could get through this. He went to Julieanna's mother's house. It was bustling with people. Victor caught a glimpse of Bridget who was warming water.
"Bridget?" Victor whispered to her.
"Sir, you know you're not supposed to be about here." She said hushed.
"What's going on?" He asked quietly.
"Today Miss Julienna and Mr. Aiden announce their engagement." She whispered to him. Victor's face went pale and he went into shock.
"Bridget YOU HAVE TO GET ME IN THERE!" Exclaimed Victor.
"But Sir, it is impossible." Said Bridget looking around at the other workers.
"Alone yes but with your help...Please. I will not hurt her. I swear." Bridget looked around and found a cloak to match one of Aidens and threw it over him. Victor handed her some coin and followed her upstairs past everyone. Mary had just walked out the door.
"Bridget, Julienna needs you." Mary said to her as she rushed by yelling at the cooks.
"Wait here a moment Sir." Said Bridget to Victor. After a moment or two Bridget ran back out.
"Go NOW Sir." Stated Bridget. Victor ran in and saw her standing by the divider. He walked over. He ran his hands down her corset. He pulled the strings on her corset. He had pulled them a little tight.
"Bridget, not so tight. I like the air in my lungs." Julienna protested. Then Victor loosened the corset some. Too much. He then pulled her hair from her neck behind her back.

"Bridget, what are you doing? Do it correctly or leave!" Julienna was becoming annoyed. He dropped the corset completely. All of her clothes pooled around her feet. Julienna, now furious, turned fast. Victor wrapped his arms around her as his lips crashed into hers. Julienna was panicked. She pulled away and covered herself.
"Julie…" Victor whispered to her as he kissed her again. Julienna, now confused, leaned in and enjoyed it. Victor's hands wandered. She wrapped her arms around him this time. He felt every crease and crevice of her body. She pulled away even though she was enjoying it.
"Victor, I've missed you my love." She said as she pulled her undergarments back where they belonged. Victor kissed her again.
"And I you." Victor began tightening her corset to a loose fit. He still ran his hands about her body. Victor pushed her to the bed as she stifled a moan. Julienna kissed him slowly. Victor ran his fingers to her core. She grabbed his hand and pulled him away.
"I'm still not ready." She explained as she sat up.
"I know. I just wanted to be sure you would be thinking of me today." Victor exclaimed. Julienna stood up and washed herself again. Victor tightened her corset and left after placing a chaste kiss upon her. Victor took that moment to send Bridget in and snuck off the grounds. Victor talked to the carriage driver that had brought him to White River. He was to drive Julienna and Aiden to their new estate. He had the driver take him there to await their arrival in the shadows of the trees. As Victor looked around the new house he noticed there was a ribbon tied in between several trees. After a few minutes a few carriages arrived including two very fancy ones. He recognized his driver. Aiden and Aaron Crawford came out of one carriage. Mary and Julienna came out of another. There were two pathways in the snow. One

in purple and one in blue. Aiden and his father followed the blue side. Julienna and her mother followed the purple. They met up at the front door. Victor admired Julienna's dress and as he watched the ceremony. At the end of the ceremony he watched them pull away in their carriage. He could feel the hurt and anger rising within him. Aaron saw Victor and approached him. The stout man still had a flask of whisky in his hand. He felt his father place his hand upon his shoulder.

"Victor, you really shouldn't be here." Explained Aaron.

"Where else should I be father?" Asked Victor as he took his father's flask and swigged the whiskey himself. Aaron took the flask back and swigged it again as he looked at his son.

"Look son, you can't have Julienna." Aaron explained.

"I WILL father. She is not married yet. I intend her to marry ME!" Exclaimed Victor.

"You will NOT covet YOUR BROTHER'S WIFE." Aaron said sternly as he put his hand on his shoulder.

"Stop me FATHER!" Victor spat back at him as he shook his father's arm from his shoulder. Victor began to run and transformed into a wolf.

# Chapter 18

Victor ran off as his anger boiled inside of him. Remembering every moment with Julienna, missing his friends that he couldn't see anymore. He felt truly alone. Victor was confused by his duty to his mother and his love of Julienna. He needed to run and clear his head from the events that have occurred. He found himself at the Kelsey manor not knowing how or why he was even there. Watching from the brush he saw everything that Mary was doing. He heard Julienna and Bridget laughing and giggling about him and the upcoming marriage. How he wished that he could run Aiden off or just flat out remove him, but Aiden was his half brother he felt torn and helpless. There were so many roads to take and none of them lead him to a life with the women he loves. He pined for Julienna and he decided that if nothing else he will have her, even if she married another she will be his. Victor had phased back to a man and took some clothes off a clothes line and dressed. He decided a cool walk was in order.

After a long walk by the edge of the woods Victor decided to head back to the cottage there was nothing more he could

do on this night. Passing the manor he needed one more glimpse of her. Although watching Julienna only made him want her more. It was getting late and the girls were getting Julienna ready for bed. As he turned to leave he heard a noise in the bushes. Had someone noticed him? Standing as still as possible and contemplating changing form out of the bush stood Aiden watching through the window on the other end of the manor as well.
"What are you doing here?" Aiden demanded as he stepped closer to Victor.
"The same as you I suppose." Victor stated as he took a step back.
"You know she IS MY PROPERTY." Aiden exclaimed to Victor, beginning to get angry.
"Beg your pardon? What are your intentions with her?" Victor growled trying not to wake the house.
"She is mine and I will do as I see fit nor you or any other "Man" will have what is mine" Aiden bellowed. Victor's face grew red and his eyes began to match he wanted to end Aiden. He knew he had the power and strength to do so but could not hurt Julienna's future in that way. And what did he mean by "man"? Did he know more than Victor thought he knew?
"When you say it that way...Have you come to know her? I have." Victor asked, not really wanting to know the answer. He couldn't stand the thought of Aiden touching his Julienna.
"You Sir are not welcome here and if you do not leave I will wake the house and ring the constable." Aiden stared at Victor trying to intimidate him. Victor, not affected by his threat, decided to accept his challenge. He looked him over quickly to be sure he didn't have a pistol on him. When he realized he was safe he began to confront and engage in a fight with him. Aiden, not prepared for Victor deciding to chase him off the property, ran to the woods to find an

advantage. Victor chased after Aiden looking for a place to phase he found a tall patch of brush as he changed to the wolf.  He jumped from the brush  snarling with bared teeth. Aiden jumped away afraid the beast was going to get him. Victor chased him from the property to his father's lavish estate.

Aiden ran through the front door trying to get away from the dog. Ripping the door open and  smashed against the wall making a hole where the knob hit.  Aiden screaming WOLF at the top of his lungs, Aaron came flying out of his quarters. Victor fled as Aiden ran into the house.  If he could have laughed in that form he would have.
"WHAT IN THE DEVIL IS GOING ON HERE?!"  Aaron screamed as he dropped a bottle of scotch from the commotion.  Aiden now on the top of the sofa with a pillow between his legs and blood dripping from his face.
"Is..Is...it gone?"  Aiden looking slowly around the room trying to decide if he should move from his perch.
"Boy have you gone mad?"  Aaron went over to see the hole the knob made and took a large swig of his drink.
"I could have been killed by that beast and you care only for that SCOTCH."  Aiden said as he stormed over to the liquor cabinet and threw all the alcohol from it.  He couldn't help but smile after seeing all the broken glass on the floor. Victor watching from a distance wanted to bust into the hall and confront his father.  But ended up deciding against it and went home.  He couldn't wait to see how this turned out. Victor layed down to sleep.  He smiled as he couldn't get the look of  Aiden's face outta his mind.  He laughed as he slowly fell asleep.   Victor began to dream. There were two boys running outside of a glorious house.  Victor recognized himself as a boy.  He had no memory of the other boy.  He kept hearing the other boy say 'come play in the woods.'

The closer Victor got to the woods the further away the other boy and the glorious house went. He could no longer smell the lilacs. He heard the stream far off in the distance. He heard barking and growling. Animals sounding all around him. He saw his mother and a quaint little cottage in a clearing. The boy kept calling him back. A woman took the boy away and forbade him from playing with Victor. “He's not like us.” The boy's mother kept saying. A great beast ran from the cottage after the woman. Victor woke up. He was covered in sweat. Victor remembered the burning red eyes of the beast. Victor saw the cave. His date with Julienna as Victor walked near the river.

“Watch that edge..It can be slippery.” said a voice from behind him. Victor turned to see a boy. The boy from his dream.
“How is this possible?” Victor asked the boy.
“It's your memory. You came here after mother chased the boy's mother away. Do you not remember? There was blood everywhere.” The boy said.
“I remember nothing. Nothing of my past. I only wish for my future. MY future with HER.” Victor said to the boy as he pointed to Julienna.
‘She has no future with you Victor. No woman does.” The boy started with a smug smile on his face.
“Who are you to tell me my future boy!” Victor yelled angrily as he moved towards the child. As Victor got to the boy he changed. The boy laughed as he turned into a dark version of Victor.
“She will never have you. She will become like you and turn away after she kills everything she loves. Namely YOU.” The evil Victor laughed.
“Wake up…!!” Julienna shook Victor. He jumped with a start. Victor looked around frantically.
“The boy...where's the boy!!?” Victor exclaimed.
“What boy Victor?” Julienna asked as she wrapped her arms around him trying to calm him down.
“The boy he was there...by the wall.” Victor pointed towards the cave walls.
“It was a dream my darling.” Julienna was still trying to get him to relax.
Victor began to breathe a little easier after looking around. His eyes had gone back to their normal shade of brown. He wrapped his arms around Julienna and did not want to let her go.
“I am so sorry that it has come to this.” Victor apologized to Julienna.
“It’s okay Victor. It was merely a dream.” Julienna said.

“Dream or not, you shall not be harmed again. Come my love I shall take you home.” Victor said. Victor woke up. The dream felt so real. Almost as a memory. As he tried to focus he heard some rustling in the house. He got out of bed to see what was going on. Thinking a racoon or something had gotten into the kitchen he had grabbed a large branch that he kept in his room and carried it over his shoulder. He found a woman going through his pantry and was about to club her with the branch until she turned around.

“Mother?? What are you doing here?” He asked as he dropped the branch.

“Just getting a few essentials. My son, were you going to hit me with that?” She pointed at the branch now on the floor.

“No Mother of course not.” Victor said as he kicked the branch away.

“Son?Mother, you said Aaron is my father?" Victor dragged out as he stepped away from his mother.

"What? I never said that." Lenore dodged the statement.

"You most certainly did mother. You may have slipped but you are saying that Aiden is my half brother." Victor said loudly. Lenore looked at him appalled. She placed her hand over her heart and gasped.

"Don't pretend to be shocked now." Victor said disapprovingly.

"I remember what happened to his mother. You killed her." Victor screamed at her as he pointed his finger at her.

"I did no such thing…" Lenore whispered as she stumbled backwards. Lenore tripped over some clutter amongst the debris. Victor stormed out the cottage. He began running and morphed into a great mighty wolf. He stopped at the top of the hill huffing. His mother chased him. Lenore caught him. Victor growled at her.

"Victor...Please!" Lenore exclaimed. Victor growled again and snapped at her as he ran off again.

## Chapter 19

*Victor,*

*I have received a wedding invitation from Anna. I would like to go but I can't be seen. If you will come with me as my friend I would very much appreciate it. It will be within a few days.*

*Always your friend,*
*Rebekah K.*

Upon reading the letter Victor decided that he had no problem going to get Rebekah. After all he was looking forward to meeting her sister she always talked so much about. Deciding to take the carriage in case anyone else would like to come to his cottage he went to the stable and prepared to leave. Packing his things he would leave tomorrow. It was a fortnight's journey so he would not need to pack too much and he really wasn't too keen on seeing his mother right now anyways. Mother meant well but she was always quite bothersome.

After closing his trunk he noticed that there was a lot of wear on it. So he had decided that while he was in White River he would stop in and pick up some new luggage. It was high time he got a hat as well. Victor went down to the silver mine and had his minors give him pouches of silver. He wore gloves to handle the pouches and traded the silver for gold. After all of his running around he had tired himself out, he ate his meal and went to bed. Victor awoke to pounding on his door. He rubbed his eyes and realized how late it was. He jumped out of bed throwing on clothes as he ran to the door.
"I'll be right out. The luggage is right inside the door." Victor shouted as he grabbed a few blankets and ran towards the door.
"Victor? Where are you going?" Lenore yelled as Victor ran out the door ignoring her. The driver of the carriage reached around the two of them grabbing bags.
"Sir is the lady coming as well?" Asked the driver as he just helped her exit the carriage.
"No she is not!" Said Victor as he looked at his mother and boarded the carriage. Lenore, upset tried to stop the driver.
"Push on I am late as it is." Exclaimed Victor as they began the ride to White River. Victor was In and out of sleep and thinking about his friend. He reached in his pocket and pulled out a set of heart shaped ruby earrings that he had made for her before Daniel's death. It was to be an engagement present for her; he felt it would bring his friendship closer. Victor loved Rebekah. She was his best friend. He put them back into his pocket wrapped safely within a silk handkerchief.

His mind went back to his mother. He wondered how angry she would be towards him as he gave her no explanation and just left. After much worrying and thinking he had finally reached White River. Knowing that his mother was not home he had the driver take him there. The carriage came to a stop and the driver unloaded his stuff. Upon placing the luggage on the porch the handle broke off the trunk and the latch opened, all of his clothes fell out onto the floor.

"Sir I am so sorry." Said the apologetic driver as he tried to pick them up.

"It's okay. Leave it." Said Victor annoyed as he pulled the driver away from the mess of clothes. Victor hastily opened the front door and threw everything on the floor. Trunk and all. He ran back into the carriage after shutting the door.

"Can you take me into town please?" Victor asked the driver.

"Sure thing." The driver said. Victor jumped back into the carriage and they took the short drive into town. Victor had been gone for months but not much had changed. All the vendors were still selling their things and Jonathan's booth was still the last one in the back. Victor walked slowly amongst the other shoppers. He found and bought two new trunks and asked to have his initials put on them. Then he bought a new suit for the wedding. It was black with a red button down shirt and a black jacket. He also bought a top hat to match. Then he walked up to Jonathan's booth.

"Hello Jonathan." Smiled Victor as he eyed some jewelry that Julienna and his mother would like.

"Victor! How de heck is ya. I ain't seen ya in a coons age!" Jonathan bellowed as he laughed.

"I'm good Jonathan." Victor said as he reached out to shake his hand.

"Boy! what is ya doin? No way is we chakin duh hand." Jonathan exclaimed as he went around the booth giving him a bear hug. Victor grunted in pain. This man even though shorter than him could squeeze the life of you.
"Whatcha doin' ere boy?" Jonathan asked.
"I'm picking up Rebekah for Anna's wedding." Victor smiled at Jonathan.
"Who be Anna?" Jonathan asked as he looked questionly at Victor.
"Who's Anna? Your niece...Rebekah's sister?" Explained Victor.
"Ya mean Julienna?" Jonathan asked.
"Anna is Julienna, Rebekah's sister?" Asked Victor.
"Suren is." Exclaimed Jonathan as he began laughing. Victor suddenly got nervous not knowing what to say. Victor grabbed the necklaces and reached into his pocket handing Jonathan some coins.
"Where's Rebekah again?" Victor asked as he put the necklaces in his pocket.
"She be at the school in that der private house on side der." Said Jonathan as he tried to point out directions with his hands full.Victor stood silently as Johnathan continued to talk, not really sure about half of what Johnathan was saying he began to wonder when Rebekah was going to be ready. Victor thanked Jonathan again and went to the school. As he arrived on the grounds he walked around and found the house that Jonathan was talking about. He walked up and knocked on the door.
"Just a minute." Shouted the familiar tone of Rebekah's voice. After a moment or two Rebekah answered the door with a white crochet shawl wrapped around her shoulder and waist.
"Rebekah. It is so good to see you again." Stated Victor as he wrapped his arms around her and hugged her. Feeling a

bump on her belly he gave her a weird look. She turned her head in shame.
"I suppose we need to talk?" Victor said more as a question.
"I suppose so. Come on in." Said Rebekah as she closed the door behind them. Victor sat on the sofa as Rebekah disappeared in the kitchen and returned with tea for them. She sat down and wrapped herself in her shawl deeper.
"Well I won't beat around the bush. Your pregnant huh? Who's the father? Daniel?" Victor said as he got up looking for something stronger to drink.
"Victor sit. I don't have any whisky, obviously!" Rebekah said sternly. Victor reluctantly sat back down completely on edge.
"No it wasn't Daniel. It was a man from my town. In Hecla." Explained Rebekah.
"What was his name?" Asked Victor.
"His name doesn't matter. The baby and I will be taken care of." Said Rebekah.
"WHAT"S THE NAME REBEKAH?" Victor pushed feeling the wolf rage within.
"Aiden. Aiden Cra…" Rebekah said quietly, not even getting his full name out before Victor rose to his feet shouting.
"CRAWFORD! THAT ARROGANT STUBBORN SPOILED POMPOUS ASS! Victor stormed around the room throwing his tea cup and many other things. The wolf inside could not be controlled.
"Victor...Vict..How could you know him? Try to talk to me." Rebekah tried to get his attention while avoiding the flying objects.
"How do you know Aiden?" Rebekah shouted to get his attention.
"DO NOT MENTION THAT NAME TO ME!" Victor shouted back as he pointed a finger at Rebekah then ran his hand

through his hair pulling it gently. Rebekah turned as the tears started to well in her eyes.
"We were to be married a month prior. We had a chaperoned date and the chaperone never showed. One thing lead to another." Rebekah explained as she held her growing belly.
"Did you love him?" Victor asked as he wished to take the thoughts from his mind.
"I loved Daniel more but it was an arranged marriage. What was I to do?" Rebekah asked as she began to cry.
"Marry Lucifer at least you know he's the devil." Victor said as he wiped her tears. Rebekah smiled at the thought. Victor sat back down and leaned into the back of the sofa covering his head.
"What about this wedding then? Are you going knowing the situation you are in? What about your family?" Victor had so many questions. She is his best friend and no matter what he will support her.
"I want to see my sister Anna married. I know that he loves her. It should work." Rebekah said as she smiled.
"You mean your sister JULIENNA?" Victor asked and he loudly boasted her name.
"How do you...?" Rebekah started to ask.
"I love her. I've been trying to sabotage the arranged marriage for a while. All the while I knew your sister Anna was messing with some suitor. I never realized I was the suitor." Victor had an epiphany as he rolled his eyes.

# Chapter 20

Arriving an hour or so before the wedding Rebekah and Victor had talked about how her family did not want her there. How Aaron Crawford sent her gold to keep her home. Rebekah had written Julienna a letter and asked Victor to give it to her at the wedding.
"I will not attend the wedding. I will be around though." Said Victor annoyed.
"My sister sent me the invitation for my friend and I." Rebekah begged.
"I will go to the reception. Only to give her the letter. This is a funeral If I should say so not a wedding." Victor said smugly.
"Fine then." Said Rebekah agitated. Victor laughed at her as he had the driver drop him off at the cottage. The carriage went off to the wedding.
Victor changed out of his suit and into something for a reception. He did not wish to stick out like a sore thumb. After a little while he combed his hair and went to the stalls to readied his horse. Upon approaching Aiden and Julienna's home again he tied up his horse and snaked

through all the people.  The thought of it being their home sickened him. He ran into Rebekah in the shadows.
"She saw me Victor."  Rebekah said happily.  He hugged his friend.
"I will only be a moment.  The horse and carriage is near the tall trees in the back.  Wait for me."  Victor said as he pointed in that direction.
"I will."  Rebekah said as she found her way back towards the shadows.  Victor again went snaking through the people until he caught sight of Julienna.  She was absolutely stunning.  Victor smiled wishing today was their day.  He made his way over to Julienna seeing that someone had just accidentally spilt wine over her beautiful dress.  He grabbed her arm and pulled her into the kitchen.  Victor used a napkin to blot the spot where the wine was spilt.
"How did this happen?  Did Aiden?"  Victor asked horsley.
"No my friend Margaret bumped me.  No harm done." Julienna stuttered.
"Then why are you shaking?"  Victor asked although he knew the answer.
"There are too many people here Victor.  Do you know how much I want to embrace you?  People will talk if they see you assisting me!"  Julienna stated.  Victor looking down pointed to her dress for her to see. Julienna looked around to make sure no one could see them.

"The stain is gone.  Thank you Victor."  Said Julienna as she ran her hand down his arms.  Their eyes met.  Victor pulled her hand away.
"No the stain is still here but believe me when I say he won't be for long.  I would say congratulations but we both know I don't mean it!"  Victor kissed her forehead as he slipped her the letter and abruptly left.  Victor dodging people makes his

way to the carriage and an excited Rebekah. She was just talking away about the wedding.
"You really do not need to share the details." Victor said glad that he didn't see Aiden. The driver had just gotten back to the carriage when the door opened. Both Victor and Rebekah looking out the door.
"You two are not supposed to be here!" Said the short pompous man.
"She is her sister! How can she not?" Victor said to his father.
"Be that as it may, she was told not to come and you my son are aware as to why you can't be here." Aaron said exasperated. Rebekah looked at Victor stunned.
"Now who's keeping secrets Victor?!" Rebekah asked, still in shock. Victor glanced over and raised his hand to her, shushing her immediately.
"We are leaving. Noone saw us." Victor said as he motioned the driver.
"We will speak of this later boy!" Aaron shouted as the carriage pulled away.
"Who was that father?" Asked Aiden as he was running up to the carriage before it left.
"Just a couple crashers. Nothing to worry about Aiden." Aaron said as he pushed Aiden back into the party with his guests.

# Chapter 21

On the carriage ride back to drop Victor off Rebekah and Victor argued the whole time.
"How can you not tell me that Aiden was your brother."
Rebekah shouted at him.

"Probably the same way you didn't tell me Julienna was your sister." Victor said back rubbing his temples.
"I talked of my sister all the time." Rebekah spat out.
"Yes your sister ANNA! No mention of the name JULIENNA!" Victor's anger began to grow.
"Look I'm sorry. Obviously we had a lot of communication barriers. Can we just stop fighting and go back to being friends with issues." Rebekah realized she needed her best friend. Victor pulled Rebekah into his shoulder and held her.
"I'm sorry too." Said Victor simply as he wrapped her back up with her shawl. The carriage came to a stop and Victor got out of the carriage. HE ran into the cottage and grabbed drinks and snacks for Rebekah.
"Here this is for the ride home. You must eat." Said Victor as he handed her the food and she placed his hand on her belly.
"This baby has a strong kick." Smiled Victor.
"Yeah he does. Maybe I'll name him Daniel." Smiled Rebekah. Victor laughed with her. The carriage pulled away again leaving Victor alone. Victor walking into the house sat at the table with parchment and ink and began writing a letter.

*Mother,*

*It has been a long time since we last spoke. In my time of need you were not around. I am very angry with you and I feel so alone and lost. For many years you lied to me never telling me of my father or my brother who now feel like are my enemies. Since I have not seen you I wish to keep it that way for a while. I will write to you if not just show up on your doorstep when I am ready. I need to sort out MY LIFE and the direction in which it is going.*

*A l w a y s,*

*Victor Wolf.*

Feeling satisfied Victor walked down to the cave and left his note for Lenore to find. As he was walking back up someone had reached out and grabbed him. Victor jumped, reaching around and pinning them to the ground. After his eyes adjusted he saw the fear in her eyes. It was Julienna, but it wasn't her. She was beginning to phase. Her blue

eyes began to turn red. She was still wearing her wedding dress.
"Victor. Please! What is happening to me?" Julienna pleaded pulling at him.
"Julienna please calm down my love." Victor tried to reassure her. Pulling her up from the floor of the underbrush he wrapped his arm around her waist and carried her to his house. Figuring that if she destroyed his home at least she would be safe. Upon entering he laid her down on his bed and let her rest for a few minutes.
"The ointment didn't work." Said Victor to himself. Julienna was now screaming from the pain. Victor went into the room with her. He took her hand looking at it phasing.
"What do I do? Please help me." Julienna begged as the tears streamed down her face. Victor began crying too.
"I need you to breathe my love. I know it hurts." Victor said as he showed her how.
"I'm not in labor you great buffon!" Screamed Julienna as she growled.
"I know you're not. BREATHE THROUGH THE PAIN!" Exclaimed Victor as he was trying to keep from phasing himself. Julienna began breathing hard. Her inner wolf took over ripping off the wedding dress. The corset blew open and she phased into a wolf growling and snarling. Victor could no longer control his inner wolf and phased as well. Julienna took off through the woods Victor chasing after her. She could hear the constable in the distance calling her name, but she continued to run. She ran to her mother's home. Victor was unable to keep up. When he finally caught up with her and watched in horror as Julienna in wolf form burst through the door ripping it off the hinges. Growling and snarling baring her teeth at anyone who dared to look at her. The servants all ran out of the house trying to get away. She saw her mother come out of her room

demanding what was going on. The wolf in her lunged at Mary attacking her in full force until she no longer moved. Julienna phased back looking down at her mother.
"You made me! YOU MADE ME MOTHER! You made me marry that man knowing all the while I was in love with Victor!" Screamed Julienna then she passed out. Victor phased back and went over to Julienna picking her up he carried her to his cottage and put her dress back on her and then getting a horse placing her upon the stead while he sat behind her holding her upright. He rode to her home. Upon arriving Victor found that no one was there. He placed Julienna on her bed. He kissed her not wanting to leave her this way but realizing he had no choice. Victor looked back at her and left unknown his brother had been outside and had seen him leave. Victor mounted his horse and went home. When he arrived he had cleaned up the house yet again. He wanted clarity and decided to phase again. He just needed to run.

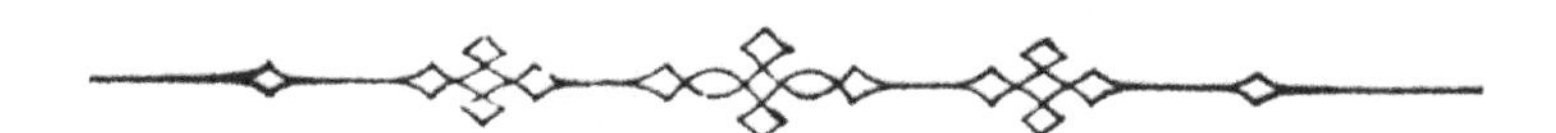

# Chapter 22

Six months later

“Julienna? I don't wish to sneak around any longer. I want a family with you.” Victor said as he rolled onto his side to look at Julienna.
“We can't. I have had no relations with him.” Julienna smiled.
“It is a dead giveaway if you are not with him. Annul the marriage. Your mother is dead and there is no reason to keep up the ploy.” Victor encouraged her.
“I...I can not have relations with him. The thought makes me ill.” Julienna gagged.
“Besides, it is winter. I need you to keep me warm.” Julienna joked as she reached for Victor and kissed him repeatedly.
Victor pulled himself from the bed and wrapped a large white blanket around himself. Julienna watched and pouted.
“Come Victor, lie back down with me.” Julienna pouted more.“I am to leave. There is no reasoning with you now.” Victor scolded.“What do you mean?” Julienna

protested."You have your house, your money and your last name. You will not bear him a child because Rebekah bore him one." Victor scolded louder."Not so loud he will hear you." Julienna protested. She got out of bed and wrapped herself with Victor in the blanket.
"It's you I love. I don't care about the money, or the name." Julienna said."The house???
" Victor asked jokingly"It's got its flaws. It's not big enough." Julienna joked and laughed. Victor shifting in the blanket still standing beside the bed.
"Does that mean..?" Victor asked"That I will annul mine and Aiden's..Aiden!!!" Julienna looked to the open door stunned to see her husband. Victor jumped away from the bed as did Julienna. Aiden remained as calm as he could considering the circumstances.
"Julienna, get out of this room now." Aiden stared at Victor. A dead calm. Victor had never feared anyone before now. Aiden walked towards Victor. Victor struggled to keep balance as he threw his clothes about him. Aiden stopped dead in front of him.
"HOW DARE YOU!?" Aiden Slapped Victor in the face. The bruise was almost instant. Victor looked onto him."I...I love..." Victor stuttered with blood from his nose and mouth.
"YOU WILL NOT DARE TO SAY THOSE WORDS! SHE IS MY WIFE." Aiden screamed and continued more calmly. "And I did not believe that you are stupid enough to bed her...IN MY OWN HOUSE!!" Aiden lost control. He jumped after Victor. Victor dodged and Aiden landed on the floor. Victor grabbing all his might began to fight back. Julienna wrapped a sheet around her and she jumped onto Aiden's back as Aiden had Victor pinned under him. Aiden threw Julienna off him. Victor and Aiden were still trying to throw punches at one another. Victor pinned Aiden to the floor growling. His brown eyes now red. He lifted Aiden's head

only to drop him back to the floor again. It was then Aiden noticed something about Victor. The boy that used to be at his home growing up.

"You have no idea of what I could do to you Aiden..." Victor smiled smugly as he got up off him. Aiden walked to his wife and put his hand out for her to take. She looked at it but she slapped it away. Aiden simply looked at them.

“You will take my hand MY wife and get off the floor!” Screamed Aiden. Again Julienna refused to take his hand as she shook her head no.
“Be gone within the hour Victor or I will call the constable..” Aiden threw a towel on the floor to Julienna as she sat still on the floor crying, bleeding from her forehead.
“Clean yourself. We will speak of this... betrayal when I return!” Aiden scorned her and left. Victor went to Julienna. He pulled her up from the floor. His red eyes now had started to turn back to brown with red streaks in them. He was physically hurt worse than Julienna but treated her wounds.
“Care for yours. I merely have a bump.” Julienna said smugly
.“I'm fine. You however...I'm so sorry...” Victor held her while she sobbed.It wasn't before long Victor was completely healed. His eyes had gone back to normal.
“You must go before he returns. I do not want anything to happen to you, please” Julienna exclaimed.
“I will not leave you alone with that man!” Victor exclaimed.
“You must go. I'll send for Margaret.” Julienna said calmly as she was pushing Victor out the door.
“I will get Margaret for you. She will be here in a few minutes.” Victor pushed his way back in the doorway. He wanted to kiss her to take her from this horrible place.
“Gather some things and hide them. I will be back for you soon.” Victor placed his hand to her forehead assessing her bump. Julienna flinched as he did. Although she knew she was already in trouble, she kissed him anyway. He kissed her back. Victor left and ran to town. Margaret had lived alone for some time and Julianna had pointed out the house several times. Running up the stairs trying not to slip on the ice he began to pound on her door. A frazzled Margaret answered the door.
“Who are you? What do you want?” Maragret asked, panicked.
“I am Victor. Go to Julienna now, please hurry before Aiden returns.” Victor blurted out in a single sentence.

"Is she alright." Margaret opened the door fully now stepping out.
"GO. She will tell you everything." Victor said as he ran off to pack things.

Arriving at Aiden's home thirty minutes past the hour Vicor could hear the shouting from the road. As there were several people at the doorway he placed his luggage down outside the door. He listened as the constable pounded on the door. Victor heard Margaret again.
"You don't get to hurt my best friend and get away with it." Margaret laughed at him. He heard a huge crash. Had Aiden attacked someone? The constable kicked open the door and shot a single round into the air. No one saw Victor or Aaron walk in from behind him. Aaron holding a bottle of scotch.
"AIDEN WHAT IS THE MEANING OF THIS?!!" the constable was very loud and angry. After the initial shot the constable managed to get his arms on Aiden. He tied his hands up and forced him into the armchair that was now set up right. Victor attended Margaret as to not enrage Aiden any further, while Mr. Crawford attended his daughter in law.
"Now, let's all have a seat and sort this mess out." stated the constable.
"Sort what mess out? If I had hurt a woman, ANY woman I would be sent to the jail. But because he did it he's going to sit here in his fancy house and get told...it's okay Aiden don't do it again?!" shouted Victor to the constable and Aaron.
"Now Victor..." Aaron started.
"Yes, now brother, listen to father. He probably told you to bed my wife." Aiden mocked.
"You worthless piece of..." Victor had enough of Aiden's mouth. He punched him in the face. His eyes now on fire.
"Brother...Father??" Julienna fainted from everything going on. Margaret had reached out and steadied her the best she could. Margaret tapping on Julienna pulled Julienna out of her spell.
"Aiden, I know we chatted some tonight about your...issues." Aaron started but was interrupted.

“Issues, Father...Ugh just lock me up, because I'd rather be there than here right now.” Aiden said as he looked at Julienna. The constable got up and walked him to the door where Aiden stopped and looked back at Julienna.
“Please MY wife. Be here when I get back. You know I didn't mean to hurt you.” Aiden pleaded with his wife.
“Constable please a moment with my wife?” Aiden begged.
“Under the circumstances...” the constable started to say yes, but Victor interrupted him.
“I will see you brother.” Victor smiled at him and waved.
Julienna seeing the whole mess, and hearing her husband plead to her put down her suitcase and for the briefest moment. She followed the men out to the patty wagon. She reached into the carriage and took Aiden's hand.
“Will you be here tomorrow my darling?” Aiden asked her with tears welling in his eyes.
“I don’t think I will.  I am going to spend time with my family.” Julienna answered and kissed her husband.
“Don’t leave me. Especially not for HIM.” Aiden pleaded as he stared at Victor.
Julienna felt a hand on her shoulder. She watched the patty wagon pull away and felt for the first time the sting of tears welling into her eyes for Aiden. She covered the hand on her shoulder with hers. Realizing it wasn't Margaret or even Victor. It was Aaron's.  Victor walked into the house after watching the wagon pull away.
After talking to Aaron Julienna walks into her house and see’s Victor poking at the fire. She walked up to him and put her hand on his back. Victor turned around and embraced her.
Julienna and Victor sat on the floor in front of the grand fireplace. A cup of hot tea in front of both of them. They were taking sips and chatting. Victor held her hand as he looked over her bruise. He gently kissed it. Julienna looked down at the floor. For once she didn't know who she wanted.
“You're my brother in law?” Julienna asked as well as she could without laughing.

“Yeah, I guess. That is probably why I haven't killed him yet.” Victor joked back as he wrapped his arms around her. Julienna more confused now had pulled away.
“What's wrong my love?” Victor is now concerned for her. Wondering if she was questioning her love for him.
“I just...I don't know my place now. When I met you it was different. You are so kind and wonderful. Aiden, I have known all my life. He has been with another woman and father's my...Rebekah's...” tears welled up as she thought of her sister. Victor looked into her eyes and smiled.
“She's happy my love.” Victor smiled at her and pulled out another letter. He put it sealed in front of her.
“I was to give it to you earlier, before everything else happened.” Victor put the letter in her hands.
“It's not right. How do you get to know if she's happy? She's my sister.” Julienna started with a weak smile and tears streaming down her face.
“Read it my love. It will bring you comfort.” Victor kissed her bruise and walked upstairs to clean the mess in the bedroom so Julienna wouldn't have to.

Julienna walked up the stairs to her bedroom to be sure that Victor was ready to go. He had on his heavy clothes and a wool blanket over his arm.
“I am ready to go my love, are you ready to go see the repairs to my cottage?” Victor asked.
Julienna took his hand and they headed towards the road to wait for the carriage. As they waited, they sat on a log outside.The snow was now heavy and it seemed it was here to stay. Julienna looked at Victor waiting for him to say something...anything, the silence was deafening. After what felt like hours, in the cold the carriage finally arrived. The driver went around to open the door for them.
“Terrible night to be out in this.” The driver explained.
“Terrible night all the way around.” muttered Julienna.
The driver closed the door behind them and was back up on the carriage. He shouted to his horses. The carriage was on its way. Julienna wrapped in tight next to Victor who was still fidgeting with his cufflinks.

"Julienna surely by now you've noticed things about me. Things you can't explain." Victor said as he ran his fingers through her hair.
"What are you trying to say? Have you changed your mind? Do you not want to be with me any longer?" Julienna asked.
"No, nothing like that. He stalled trying to find the right words. I am still very much in love with you but it's hard to explain. I guess the only thing I can do is come out and say it." He fumbled a bit with the cufflinks on his shirt sleeve then pulled the blanket around them tighter hugging her as it snowed harder. He didn't know how to tell her and feared she would not accept him. He finally looked up at Julienna. She grabbed his hands.
"Tell me my love." Julienna insisted.
"I'm...different. Well I'm well... ummm" Victor stalled.
"Come now it can't be that bad." Julienna pressed.
"I'm a werewolf..." Victor leaned into Julienna's ear and whispered as tears filled his eyes.
"You're the beast! A werewolf." Julienna exclaimed as she covered her mouth with her hands.
"As are you now... my love." Victor said knowingly as a tear fell from his eye onto his cheek.
"But how I mean when did you know." asked Julienna.
"Aiden did not lie to you. It was you that attacked your mother." Victor explained.
"But I would never do that. No matter what mother did to me." Said Julienna.
"Julienna, I would not lie to you, I saw it with mine own eyes. You came to me that night my love. It was your first time changing. You were much faster than I... I...could not stop you." Victor hung his head in shame. Julienna not knowing what to say or do simply covered her eyes and began crying once again.
"Where are we going?" She managed through tears.
"A quick stop to my mother's house. Quick being eight hours away. You may as well get some rest." Said Victor as he covered her with another blanket. She was in his arms and she was safe now nothing else mattered.

“And then a swing to Huron, South Dakota. I have purchased an estate there a few months ago.” Stated Victor. Realizing she was already asleep he had closed his eyes and dozed off too.

# Chapter 23

The ride took a little longer than eight hours due to the snow storm. The driver had to pull over and get into the carriage with them. After an hour or so and checking periodically on the horses.

“Maybe we should give the horses a rest for the night.” The driver looked to Victor for guidance. “Absolutely I want those horses comfortable and warm. Build them a fire to let off the chill.” Victor advised the driver. Looking over to Julienna as she continued to sleep.

“Do you need help?” Victor asked, not wanting the poor man in the cold.

“Sir no. A gentleman of your stature…besides you should tend to the lady” the driver suggested.
“Sir I am a bastard born blessed with a fine education. I have no problem helping to pull my weight.” Exclaimed Victor as he stepped out into the cold. Reaching out of the carriage trunk Victor pulled many large logs out and placed bark below it while the driver dug a hole in the snow. It wasn’t long before a roaring fire was going. The horses lied beside it, needing sleep. The snow was pushed away. Victor awoke Julienna.
“My love. We had to stop but we started a fire. Would you like to be warm?” Victor asked her sweetly. Julienna said nothing, she merely nodded her head. VIctor escorted her out of the carriage and to a log that he and the driver placed nearby. As the storm had passed the horses woke anxious and ready to move on before the next storm came through and got them packed up and ready to get back on the road. He helped Julienna back into the carriage and helped the driver prepare to leave as well. Once back on the road a couple hours more and they had arrived at Victor’s mother’s home.
“Please return promptly in the morning.” Said Victor to the driver.
“Sir I have never been out this way. Where may I stay.” Asked the driver.

“Down the road about a mile is an inn with a stable. They are very kind. Tell them I sent you and the bill will be under Aaron.” Explained Victor.
“Your father Sir?” The driver confirmed
“Yes. He wasn’t so kind to me.” Explained Victor as he smirked. The driver nodded and left. Victor walked up to the door. He wasn’t sure how his mother would feel since his last letter. He decided to knock since he no longer lived here. Jonathan opened the door.
“Victor! MA BOY Mighty good to see ya but ya shouldn’t have come all this way wit out a letter er somethin’.” Jonathan pushed him back from the doorway. He wasn’t as loud as he normally was and Victor could tell that something was off about Johnathan like he was trying to hide something.
“Is my mother sick? What is wrong?” Victor began to panic.
“NAW ya mother ain’t sick...She’s well ow do I put it?” Jonathan tried to explain. Victor grew impatient and pushed by him. Victor found Lenore on her bed. Her hair was white and she was aging much faster than normal.
“Mother what has happened to you?” Victor begged her for an answer.
“ I’m aging my son. I was nearly thirty when I had you. As I age because of the phasing I am in constant pain.” Lenore explained as Jonathan and Julienna walked into the room. Victor wiped away a stray tear.
“Will you be alright mother? A doctor perhaps?” Victor suggested.
“I need the pack healer. There is nothing a doctor can do for me.” Lenore said as she pulled out a picture of an old man and handed it to Victor.
“I will find him for you mother. Where must I go?” Victor jumped up.
“You must go to Huron, South Dakota. Our pack is there. Your grandfather if still alive is the pack leader.” Lenore explained as she closed her eyes and fell asleep. Victor walked to Julienna and Jonathan.

“Julienna, would you like to come with me? Or perhaps you would like to visit Rebekah?” Victor looked at Julienna with hopeful eyes praying she chooses him but knew her love for her sister.

Made in the USA
Monee, IL
06 November 2020